Secret
OF THE
Wastelands

Center Point
Large Print

Also by Bliss Lomax and available from
Center Point Large Print:

The Leather Burners
The Phantom Corral

**This Large Print Book carries the
Seal of Approval of N.A.V.H.**

Secret
OF THE
Wastelands

BLISS
LOMAX

CENTER POINT LARGE PRINT
THORNDIKE, MAINE

This Center Point Large Print edition is published
in the year 2016 by arrangement with
Golden West Literary Agency.

The text of this Large Print edition is unabridged.
In other aspects, this book may vary
from the original edition.
Printed in the United States of America
on permanent paper.
Set in 16-point Times New Roman type.

ISBN: 978-1-68324-183-6 (hardcover)
ISBN: 978-1-68324-187-4 (paperback)

Library of Congress Cataloging-in-Publication Data

Names: Lomax, Bliss, 1888–1979, author.
Title: Secret of the wastelands / Bliss Lomax.
Description: Center Point Large Print edition. | Thorndike, Maine :
Center Point Large Print, 2016.
Identifiers: LCCN 2016034842| ISBN 9781683241836 (hardcover :
alk. paper) | ISBN 9781683241874 (pbk. : alk. paper)
Subjects: LCSH: Large type books. | GSAFD: Western stories.
Classification: LCC PS3507.R1745 S43 2016 | DDC 813/.54—dc23
LC record available at https://lccn.loc.gov/2016034842

Secret
OF THE
Wastelands

1

"These scientists must be discouraged, turned back—killed, if necessary!" Quan Goon said with finality, his deeply carved, hawklike face revealing an ungoverned arrogance and ferocity. "This Flagler expedition must never be permitted to explore the Pueblo Grande ruins! It means disaster for the Wu-tai-shan Company —desecration of the graves of our honorable dead!"

He was a big, powerful man, such as come only from the northern provinces. His was not the only voice in this weighty conference now ending in the sumptuous private apartment over Carlotta Soong's ornate gambling establishment in Reno's Chinatown. And yet he eyed the others fiercely, as though daring them to contradict him.

Carlotta herself, young, exquisitely beautiful, her hair as smooth and black as satin and her dark eyes with their faint almond slant giving the only hint of the Chinese blood that was in her, regarded the three men seated across the teakwood table from her with concern.

"We shall find some way to stop them." She spoke their tongue, her voice proud, scornful. "That is why I have invited them here tonight for dinner. I shall learn their plans and be able to cope with them."

The three men nodded. There was something inscrutable about them, with their parchment-yellow faces and hooded eyes. Sui Chen, ostensible head of a modest importing firm, was stout, bland and plainly as shrewd as he was pacific. Little Doy Kee resembled a hundred thousand countrymen and typified them in unshakable calm and passive acceptance of the inevitable. Together with Quan Goon, all were mature in years, though Sui Chen, at sixty, alone could claim to have reached the age of wisdom.

All held high positions in the Wu-tai-shan Company. Taking counsel together, weighing and voting and deciding, they guided its destiny. Secretly, its activities went far beyond the ownership of Carlotta's establishment and Sui Chen's importing business. News of the Flagler Foundation's archaeological expedition from the East, planning so soon to go down to the Pueblo Grande Indian ruins in southeastern Nevada for purposes of exploration, had come as a bombshell, for in that very section of the great Amargosa Desert the Wu-tai-shan Company had its richest stake, and one with whose safety and security no gambling chance was to be considered for a moment.

"Since the hour of our organizing we have made desperate efforts to keep away from the white men! It was the only hope of our people," Quan Goon concurred. "In that desolate, unwanted wasteland, and with the gracious consent of the gods, we have succeeded beyond our dreams. . . . Men die mysteriously in the desert. If these scientists persist in their folly they will be stopped before they ever lay eyes on Pueblo Grande!"

Doy Kee gravely agreed; it was the only way, he said. Sui Chen hesitated, noting the frown which flitted across Carlotta's oval face like a shadow.

"Violence is for fools," she told them. There was something magnetic, compelling, about this vital girl. Not even these impassive, Buddhalike men were wholly immune to it. It explained why she performed the business of the Wu-tai-shan Company before the world, taking care of its banking and routine affairs. "Let us be wise. Wisdom is always the better weapon. Some legal trickery might serve us. I can speak to Slade Salters. He is coming tonight." Salters was her attorney.

"No!" Quan Goon thundered. "That foreign devil must not be told anything! He has already learned too much—"

"Salters knows only what I choose to tell him, and that is little," Carlotta declared steadily. But even Sui Chen found reason to agree with Quan Goon now.

"The white lawyer must know nothing of our

interest in the scientists, lest he guess too much, little daughter. . . . Think of something else."

"That you, of all persons, should be the one to counsel soft actions!" Quan Goon burst out, gazing at her incredulously, in an access of sullen anger. "You, more than anyone, should demand vengeance of these dogs of whites—and lose no smallest chance to claim it!"

"I should hate them all," she said, thinking of the mining-camp justice that long ago had left her white mother to die on the open desert in dead of winter, "and I do hate them! It was not they who brought me up, educated me—gave me an opportunity in life—"

"A desert man has already been chosen to guide these grave despoilers," Quan Goon went on bitterly. "That man will cause us trouble!"

"Jim Morningstar," Sui Chen put in as if remembering suddenly. "He came to my store this afternoon, looking for a cook for the expedition. I did not discourage him—"

"Morningstar?" Carlotta echoed sharply, leaning forward and fixing her gaze on Sui Chen. That name meant something to her. Sui Chen nodded, without a break in the passivity of his face.

"His son."

He added what he knew of Morningstar. It was not much, but this type of desert man, hard, young and capable, was familiar to them all.

For a moment Carlotta gazed musingly off into

space as though she no longer heard. Her thoughts were busy. Presently she appeared to come to some decision.

"Doy Kee!"

"Yes, Rose-petal."

"I know you are a learned man—a greater scientist than these men who will be here this evening. But you will be their cook, Doy Kee. I will arrange it. You are a stranger in Reno."

The Chinese agreed submissively. "One does not hesitate to demean himself when it serves our interests. I will keep a watch on their activities— turn back anyone attempting to leave the ruins. Is not that what we ask?"

Quan Goon leaned forward to deliver a fierce aside. "Just be sure, Doy Kee, that you succeed well, or—"

A door opened noiselessly and a houseboy, bearing an armful of blossoms, padded softly into the room and began to arrange the blossoms in a vase that was true Ming. Another boy followed, bearing a tray of sweetmeats.

Quan Goon got to his feet and bowed. "It is late," he said. "We shall continue our discussions tomorrow."

Doy Kee followed him out. Plump Sui Chen remained at the table. His eyes followed Carlotta as she crossed the room, regal in her exquisitely embroidered jacket of imperial jade and trousers of dullest gold. The reflected glow from the porcelain lamps touched her face with a kindly finger.

"Moy Quai, you are beautiful tonight," said Sui Chen. "You were well named Rose-petal. I shudder at this Carlotta they call you."

"It was my mother's name," the girl murmured. With the careful eye of an impresario she surveyed the details of this sumptuously appointed room, rich with its embroidered hangings, its hand-carved furniture and priceless porcelains. She lit a joss paper and deposited it before the image of Kwan Yam, the Goddess of Mercy, that occupied a niche of honor in the wall. "In some quarters— behind my back, I assure you—I understand that I am called the Empress Carlotta." Her smile was without bitterness. Sui Chen winced.

"These whites have evil tongues," he said. He, too, rose to leave. "It is the Feast of the Lanterns," he murmured. "A moment for laughter and soft words, but there can be no laughter when the gods frown on us."

Carlotta stood at the window for a moment after he left. Parting the heavy damask silk curtains, she peered out at the strings of bobbing paper lanterns that decorated Chinatown. The quarter had a holiday air tonight. The street was crowded with whites and Chinese. Cowboys from the Washoe Valley ranches, their spur chains jangling on the sidewalks, miners with the muck still on their boots, were streaming into her establishment.

Few who played there had any acquaintance with her.

The sound of carriages below warned her that her guests were arriving. Slade Salters, dark, debonair, ushered them in. Her invitation had been extended through him. He introduced Dr Malcolm Birdsall, head of the Flagler expedition, and Clay Masters, up from the U.S. Mint at Carson City. Dr Birdsall himself introduced the members of his own party: Jennifer Orme, the zoologist; nervous little Balto Stubbs, archaeologist and antiquarian; tall, stocky, good-natured Bill Merriam, a geologist of note, and Hans Krock, the expedition's well-known photographer. Several members of the faculty of the University of Nevada accompanied them.

Curiosity was largely responsible for their presence, but they were hardly prepared to be received in such an atmosphere of good taste and sophistication. Carlotta read their surprise. Only in the upturned corners of her strong mouth did she reveal her contempt for these people. She held Jennifer Orme's attention for a moment.

"You excite my interest," Carlotta told her. "You are very brave to face the hardships of such a trip. You are the only woman going with the expedition?"

"Yes—but I never think of myself that way," Jennifer answered. "If I did I'd unconsciously be expecting favors. I try to take a man's view of it."

"Obviously you know nothing about a man's viewpoint," thought Carlotta. "Not that you aren't pretty enough without trying to be and despite those ugly glasses." She didn't have to be told that in Jennifer Orme's busy life there never had been any time for romance. Aloud, she said: "I'm afraid you are far too charming, Miss Orme, for any man to forget that you are a woman."

Dr Birdsall stepped forward. "Miss Soong, may I present Jim Morningstar, who's taking us to Pueblo Grande?"

Carlotta's anticipated hatred of Morningstar received a jolt as her eyes lingered on his strong, clean-boned face, stamped with unmistakable resolution; on his high, broad shoulders. He was a man at whom any woman would look twice. She knew a brief moment of disquiet even as the thought crossed her mind. As for Morningstar, he found himself gazing almost rudely at this vital, self-possessed, strangely compelling girl whom he had often heard called the Empress in cow camps and on the range. Her color, her erectness, even her unescapable mystery, everything about her had a peculiar drag for him.

"This is all very informal," Carlotta said, a flutelike note in her voice, "but I am so glad you could come. We must have a long talk later. I'm deeply interested in your plans for taking the expedition to Pueblo Grande."

He had no way of knowing how true this was.

She gave him her hand for a moment and he felt something electric pass through his fingers. "I'm afraid my work will be the least important of any," he said with his slow, engaging smile.

"You are too modest," Carlotta replied, letting him go. Hans Krock beckoned him and tried to explain the excellence of some rare Chinese prints. "They do these things better than we, Morningstar," Krock declared. "They have a simplicity of line that we have never been able to match."

After a few minutes Jim was glad to escape. He found Miss Orme at his side. He had accepted her as a practical person, unlikely to present a problem on the long trip into the desert.

"I wonder if you realize that a fortune has been spent on this room?" she queried. "I'd hesitate to name the value of that vase. And this gorgeous jade!" Her long fingers caressed a bowl of purest rose quartz. "There are so many beautiful things here," she sighed.

Morningstar heard her without listening. Thinking of Carlotta, he found the words doubly true. He glanced in her direction, only to catch her withdrawing her eyes from him.

A few minutes later a Chinese boy removed a screen from a wide archway and Carlotta led them in to dinner. Strange viands appeared, and they were delicious. Carlotta, seated at the head of the table, accepted the compliments gracefully, but it was Slade Salters who kept the conversation in full stride. Big and handsome, sure of himself and his engagingly frank smile, he was well equipped for that office.

"This is the pleasantest moment of our stay in Reno," Dr Birdsall declared. "We shall remember it for weeks."

Carlotta smiled at the unconscious irony she found in his words.

In the midst of a third course of nobly prepared duck, mandarin style, Dr Birdsall leaned forward to speak across the table. "Morningstar, if we had a cook like this we'd live high at Pueblo Grande." It was said in a bantering tone, yet Carlotta, on the alert for just such an opening, took it up at once.

"Why not this very cook?" she put in quietly, as though it were the simplest of matters. "He is my own, but I seldom make use of him except on occasions like the present. . . . There is no obligation involved whatever, Doctor," she hastened to assure, when Birdsall would have protested. To the expressionless Chinese behind her chair she said: "Wong, ask Doy Kee to step here."

Doy Kee presently made his appearance, bowing modestly. There was nothing attractive in his yellow face or blank eyes, yet Birdsall gazed on him as a veritable prize. A few swift exchanges passed between Doy Kee and Carlotta in euphonious Chinese, and then Carlotta said, lapsing into English:

"Very well. You will go into the desert with these friends of mine and cook for them, Doy Kee. They start— Is it this coming Friday, Doctor?" she broke off. Birdsall hastened to confirm her, whereupon she completed her instructions to Doy Kee smoothly and rapidly.

"All light," Doy Kee assented in a pidgin he would have scorned to use at another time. "I go like you say, missy."

"And thank you very kindly," Dr Birdsall told Carlotta warmly, as the cook turned away. "This certainly leaves us in your debt." Gazing shrewdly from one to another as he followed the exchange, Slade Salters asked himself if this was the innocent service it appeared to be and whether the scientist would have occasion later to alter his opinion. It was a suspicion based on knowledge that would have surprised Carlotta.

Meanwhile, talk of another order was going forward at the other end of the table. Clay Masters had just mentioned the interesting fact that it was now scientifically possible to recognize raw gold and to identify its source with ease. Occasionally there was an exception. Masters cited as an example the coarse gold coming into the mint in small quantities from Chinese shopkeepers, ranch cooks and other Orientals scattered through Nevada.

"Undoubtedly this gold is all alike," he declared, "and yet its origin is completely unknown to us at the mint. I sometimes amuse myself—and this will amuse you too, Miss Soong—with the fancy that some rich, unknown mine has been discovered deep in the desert and kept an absolute secret. Of course the Chinese will tell nothing. Invariably they declare they panned the gold out of some small stream in the hills—or they say 'No sabby' to every question put to them!"

He laughed at his conjecture, but Carlotta chose to find a literal question in the glance he tossed her. "It would be more interesting than amusing if true," she said lightly. "My establishment has sometimes been called a gold mine. I know nothing about any other. I'm afraid you are hunting a fantastic improbability."

Watching her, Morningstar thought how difficult it would be to question anything which fell from those lips. He would have been considerably interested to learn of the tight, cold band which closed about her heart at the turn the talk was taking. Things were indeed growing desperate. Quan Goon's plea for violence seemed harder to resist.

Slade Salters was nearer the truth. He knew Carlotta well enough to grasp something of her secret perturbation. The idea put forth by Clay Masters had never occurred to the attorney, yet it was far from a surprise. It seemed to answer a number of questions he had long asked himself.

"Perhaps the truth has been kept even from you, Carlotta," he observed quietly.

"I think not," she closed him off curtly. It was as though she wanted to be done with the subject. Getting that, even Morningstar read an undercurrent of tension here which he could not fathom. Carlotta was not easily discountenanced, however, and adroitly turned the conversation to the plans of the Flagler expedition.

It was not difficult for her to elicit the information she wanted without arousing suspicion. Only Morningstar caught the thread of tautness in her. Later, when the others ventured downstairs to try their luck at fan-tan, she successfully held him back.

"Gambling holds no fascination for me," she said. "Come, we will sit here and smoke." She placed a cigarette in a long ivory holder and held it up for him to light. Over his own cigarette Morningstar regarded her with growing interest. Life seemed to flow in her in a great sweeping tide, as though the white and yellow blood in her were ever in conflict. "Late at night, when the quarter is quiet, I often sit here and listen to the Truckee tumbling over the rocks," she murmured. "It always brings me peace."

"I've listened to that river a few nights myself," Morningstar told her. "You know, when you've lived in the desert as long as I have you don't pass a river by without looking at it twice. It means something to you . . . reminds you of the days when you would have given your right arm for a few drops of water." His tone was soft, mellow. A mood was on him to which he had long been a stranger. The nearness of this girl, the intoxicating perfume she wore, the very air of this incense-laden room seemed to put a spell on him. He threw it off and opened one of the long windows.

Carlotta watched him secretly.

"What will you do about water on this trip?" she asked.

"We'll fill the tanks in Piute. There's no water beyond there. Two days' riding will bring us to Pueblo Grande. When our supply runs low we'll have to send a wagon into Piute for more."

"You could be four days without water, if anything happened to the tanks?" Carlotta queried. "Two days going and two days coming, that is. . . . It might be a desperate situation for you."

"I'll see that nothing happens to the tanks," Jim assured her.

"I trust you will be careful," she murmured as she tapped the ashes from her cigarette. Quan Goon had said that strange things happened on the desert. After a pause she said: "I suppose you know Pueblo Grande?"

"I've seen it," he acknowledged, wondering at her interest and somehow finding a warning lying deep behind her words.

"Isn't it dangerous to wander through old ruins?" she inquired. "Don't they sometimes come tumbling down?"

Morningstar smiled. "You are not suggesting that that is what is going to happen at Pueblo Grande, are you?"

"No, the gods forbid! I was only thinking of your responsibility. The lives of these men and Miss Orme will be in your keeping. . . . I shouldn't like to see anything tragic happen."

"You are needlessly alarmed, Miss—er— Soong. I promise you I shall return them safely to Reno a few weeks hence. I know those ruins are crumbling. So does Doctor Birdsall. He has agreed that if work becomes dangerous the expedition will be called back."

"Prudence is always wise," she told him, dissembling whatever satisfaction his words gave her. "And if you find the Miss Soong difficult on your tongue—you may call me Carlotta."

She leaned toward him impulsively as she heard the others on the stairs. "Take this," she murmured earnestly. "Always keep it with you. It will bring you luck."

She placed in his hand a little jade figurine carved in the shape of a remarkably lifelike dragon.

Morningstar gazed at it for a moment, then at her, and finally his eyes came back to the little figurine. Its carving was flawless. Its value was considerable. And it was a gift from her. But somehow he read a significance into the giving of it that outweighed those considerations.

"It has claws—and they are sharp," he said.

"That is true." She spoke softly, almost with regret, it seemed. "But remember, they can protect as well as destroy!"

2

Slade Salters was tall and broad-shouldered, a handsome figure of a man, and yet somehow he appeared small in contrast with the three men who shared his office this morning. A glance told that the trio were more at home on the range than in town. But they had made themselves comfortable here, looking to the attorney as to a trusted intimate, and no wonder, for, men of unsavory repute as they were by whatever standard of judgment, not a one of them but owed his liberty at the present moment to Salters. Nor did the obligation end there. Cattle rustlers and small-time holdup men, they had constant need of the services of a not-too-particular lawyer.

"Give us an idear of what this proposition of yores is, Slade." Tip Slaughter cocked an ice-blue eye at Salters, the reddish stubble on his rocky jaw glowing like wires in the sunlight from the window.

"It's a long shot," the attorney warned, "but it's good, or I wouldn't have bothered to send for you. This Masters, from the mint, wasn't telling all he knew, but he did say there's a lot of gold that's exactly alike, turning up at the mint in small lots, and they don't know where it's coming from because the mine is not recorded. Trust a bunch of Chinks to keep a thing like that secret! There's a mine, all right, and if the pigtails have got it I aim to get it! It 'll make us all rich."

"But do yuh know where it is?" Snap Clanton demanded.

"Only that the Empress and the rest of the Wu-tai-shan Company are mighty worked up over this expedition that's going out to hunt Indian relics," was the answer. "But that's enough for me. Why, the Chinks 've even figured it out to have one of them taken along as cook." He related how Carlotta had managed that bit of business and pointed out its significance. "Where there's that much smoke, there's bound to be fire!" he declared.

"An' so yuh want us to go down there in the desert an' grub around?" Bart Cagle rasped dubiously. "Why, there's five hundred square miles uh nothin' but sand, Salters!"

"Hold on," Slaughter put in coolly at this point. "We ain't even decided there *is* a mine yet! It all sounds mighty phony to me." Clanton nodded agreement, and they waited for Slade's answer.

He responded with the story of all that had occurred at the Feast of the Lanterns' dinner; how the heads of the Wu-tai-shan Company had acted as though they had something to cover up; how Carlotta had deliberately taken Jim Morningstar's measure, and how she had declared outright that there was no mine and yet had all but snapped at him when he ventured to press her gently on the matter.

"I tell you I know what I'm talking about," he reiterated his conviction firmly. "This thing is big! More than that, this mine is somewhere near the Pueblo Grande Indian ruins."

"But we've not only got the Chinks to deal with but Morningstar too," Clanton grumbled. He knew all about Morningstar, as did the others.

"Too much for you boys to handle, is it?" Salters came back with crisp satire.

"That's all right too," the renegade retorted doggedly. "No harm in lookin' matters over from every angle. It's my guess there's dead men in this, an' it may be us!"

Slade scoffed him to silence and turned his attention to Slaughter. Tip was less impressed by the obstacles but plainly still inclined to ridicule the possibility that the mine existed at all. Salters succeeded in convincing him at length only by promising that if he followed instructions he would soon enough be forced to realize the truth.

"I'm not in this for the fun of it," the lawyer reminded, "and I don't think you are. Now, what I want you to do is this. That scientific expedition is heading south for Sodaville on Friday, and from there they'll strike into the desert for these ruins—"

Snap Clanton knew that country. "Pueblo Grande? It's somewhere over around Piute," he interrupted.

"Then you could pick up the expedition there," Salters nodded. "Follow it, and watch every move that's made. But keep out of sight yourselves, and never mind just now about the mine. Just learn all you can and I've a hunch it 'll drop into our hands when the time comes. What money you need I'll supply."

The men agreed to that plan. For some time the talk was of ways and means. At last the trio made ready to leave, and Salters lowered his voice for a final word.

"Don't misunderstand me," he told them levelly. "Do as you're told and things will go smoothly. I say that because there's plenty of chance in this business for something to go haywire. You know these Chinks, and I don't have to warn you about Morningstar. Just keep out of sight and keep your eyes open, that's all. I'll meet you in Piute in two weeks."

Under Jim Morningstar's direction the Flagler expedition struck south into the desert on schedule. Toward sunset of a sweltering day they pitched camp at the base of a high butte not more than a day's travel from Pueblo Grande.

Late in the afternoon a brisk wind had sprung up; sand blew across the open flats and rustled in the drought-twisted sagebrush. Dusk brought with it a bleakness that did little to promote good spirits. An hour later it was cold. The desert chill settled down. Even Dr Birdsall was depressed, making a wry face at the sand in his food at supper. The rest were silent or low-spoken, except for the three cowboys, Sulphur Riley, Johnnie Landers and Happy Failes—Jim's assistants— who made light of anything less than a catastrophe.

There were eleven in the party, including Morningstar. Perhaps the one member they were all most conscious of was Jennifer Orme. Even Jim kept watching her where she sat near the fire, gazing into the flames. He asked himself whether she would be able to stand up to the rigors of this trip.

Curiously enough, she showed less sign of weariness and depression than her companions. She was pretty, too, in a quiet way, Jim was forced to admit; her tendrils of honey-colored hair blew about her face in a delightful way. There was serenity in those hazel eyes. This girl was vital, however little she chose to make of the fact.

"You'll hear the coyotes howling when the wind drops." Bill Merriam endeavored to engage her in talk. Big and lazy, with a deep voice and salty common sense, he was a likable chap.

"I've heard them before," she told him. They conversed desultorily, Balto Stubbs, Dave Sprague and Hans Krock, the photographer, listening.

Morningstar was still busy with his final preparations for the night. "Better gather plenty of dry sage and keep a blaze going," he told Sulphur and the others. "It 'll get colder toward morning."

Sulphur, lank and lantern jawed, his eyes deep-set, shrewd, got to his feet, grumbling. It was just his way. "Hain't enough brush in this country to keep a blaze goin' all night," he grunted.

Jim smiled and left it at that. As he turned back to the fire something flashed down from above and buried itself in the embers. Balto Stubbs, short and stout and excitable, vented a cry of surprise. The others were no less startled.

Taking a single swift stride, Morningstar leaned down and plucked a long, wicked-looking knife out of the flames. He was just in time, for there was a paper skewered on the thin blade, its edges already beginning to curl and brown. Jim removed it and flattened it out. His face went thin and cold as he read the two words printed there. He stared at them so long that curiosity began to get the better of the others.

"What is the meaning of this business anyway?" Dr Birdsall exclaimed sharply. "What does that paper say, Morningstar?"

"It says: 'Go back,' " Jim answered simply. He held the paper out. Bill Merriam took it gingerly and examined it. But it was the knife for which Jennifer extended her hand. It passed from one to another when she was done with it. Dr Birdsall gazed at the blade long and thoughtfully, turning it over and over.

" 'Go back!' " he repeated to himself, in a tone of complete puzzlement. "Surely this warning can't have been meant for us? Why should anyone be interested in stopping us?"

"You can be sure it was meant for you," Jim advised, "even though it might have been the work of a crazed desert rat."

"There's no reason why anyone should want to stop the expedition," the doctor insisted. "There must be some mistake—"

"There's no mistake," Jim denied quietly. "People just don't come to this desolate country offhand. Until a few minutes ago I would have sworn there wasn't a man within forty miles of us."

"But doesn't the knife itself tell you anything?" Hans Krock, thin and inoffensive, with his thick-lensed glasses, queried.

"I presume it is an Indian knife," Dr Birdsall declared.

"Of course!" Professor Stubbs agreed.

28

"I'm sorry," Jennifer contradicted them. "It is a Chinese knife. See the small dragons etched on the blade here, near the haft?"

"But there are thousands of knives of Chinese make," Dave Sprague pointed out. "We may even be carrying one ourselves."

"That's true," the girl admitted readily. "I only mentioned the fact for what it is worth."

Studying her, Jim decided she was not so much frightened as entertained by all this. Not so Bill Merriam, however. "Perhaps it would be best if you were to go to your tent, Jennifer," he proposed anxiously. "There's no telling what might happen next."

"We're in no real danger," Morningstar assured him. "Whoever tossed the knife could have killed us had he wanted to. Evidently he isn't prepared to go that far."

"I still think Miss Orme is exposing herself needlessly," Merriam insisted. Jim had no trouble reading his keen interest in the girl. But just now Jim had something else on his mind.

"Doy Kee!" he called. The Chinese came forward stolidly. Both Morningstar and Dr Birdsall questioned him concerning the knife, to all of which Doy Kee answered woodenly, "No sabby." Plainly nothing was to be got out of him.

"The knife was thrown from somewhere up on the butte," the doctor said. "Let's have a look up there—"

"No use," Jim told him. "It would take time, and whoever dropped the knife would be gone before we could hope to reach him. . . . We'll move out from the butte a hundred yards and the boys will take turns standing guard. It's only a guess, but we may have come close to someone's secret, and it may not have anything to do with the ruins. We should reach Pueblo Grande before dark tomorrow. There's no occasion to be alarmed until someone tries to stop us."

It was a final word. Even Dr Birdsall made plain that he approved Jim's judgment; and yet, if the others were satisfied, Morningstar himself was not so easily pleased. He did not forget what Jennifer had said about the tiny dragons etched on the blade of that dropped knife. Unconsciously, through his trousers, his fingers followed the hard outline of the jade dragon given him by Carlotta Soong. Was there a connection here? What did it all mean?

3

There was a somber austerity about Pueblo Grande, seen under the solemn afterglow of a desert evening. Extending for more than a quarter mile beneath the shadow of a lofty cliff, the venerable ruin lay at the foot of a vast and nameless rimrock flanking the desolate Fortification Mountains. This lonely site of a bygone grandeur held the party of scientists in thrall. Only the cries of the canyon swallows, dipping and wheeling overhead, broke the heavy silence.

"We'll set up camp down here under the mesquites," Morningstar told Dr Birdsall. The doctor nodded absently, absorbed to the exclusion of all else with the prospect of imminent discoveries.

Under Jim's direction the tents were set up and the camp laid out with a view to its being a permanent base. Doy Kee soon had supper sizzling over a fire. The swift desert evening descended while they were eating. The crumbling battlements of the pueblo melted into velvet obscurity, somehow only enhancing the brooding mystery of this place. An owl's mournful hoot echoed on the rocks.

Had Dr Birdsall and his associates taken time to notice, they would have observed Sulphur, Johnnie and Happy Failes slipping quietly out of camp after a murmured word from Jim. If the others had momentarily forgotten the incident of the knife in the excitement of arriving at their destination he did not. Nothing further had been heard of the mysterious prowler who had conveyed the warning to turn back, but Jim, not disposed to let it go at that, had sent the three punchers out on a little scouting trip.

They returned late to report their failure to see anything suspicious. Morningstar felt relieved. He turned back to the fire, where several members of the expedition still lingered in restless anticipation of the morrow. One of them was Jennifer.

"I see the boys are back," she smiled at him. "I've been trying to convince myself that they didn't find anything."

He showed frank surprise at her acuteness. "It does no harm to make sure of these things," he responded lightly.

"None at all," she agreed at once. "But I want you to know I appreciate your thoughtfulness for our safety."

He watched her move toward her tent as if he had never quite clearly seen her before. Admiration and a new respect followed. "She'll make a better hand than some of these others, unless I'm pretty much mistaken," he told himself. "I thought I was moving on the quiet, but not much escapes her!"

Morning saw the work of exploration begun at the ruins. With one or two exceptions these scientists were like children in their utter pre-occupation with their work. For it was work of the hardest kind, slaving and grubbing amid dirt and decay for uncomplaining hours on end to recover a single broken dish or a few beads belonging to an earlier period, all the while totally oblivious of the life about them. Morningstar soon saw that he could never trust them to scent threatened danger of their own accord, though its shadow were thrown at their very feet.

Nor was he mistaken. The long desert day drew out to a hundred fascinating finds, announced by repeated shouts of enthusiasm echoing weirdly from these walls of the dead; evening had come, and the tired, dirt-stained archaeologists were about to quit when a sudden muffled rumble and tremor rolled through the mud-walled passages. A puff of dust in Jim's face, as if blown from a giant bellows, warned him what to expect. Even as he sprang toward the spot from whence it came there was a second, and louder, rumble. A yell rang out. The next moment he saw a whole section of the ruins crumbling down, wall after wall toppling forward, the fog of dust so thick and strangling that the trapped explorers could not see which way to turn.

Jim saw Balto Stubbs rushing away with some ancient treasure in his arms, forgetting his associates in his concern for the object. Then Dr Birdsall stumbled into him.

"For God's sake, Morningstar, this is terrible!" he gasped. "Can't something be done to stop it?"

Jim thrust him aside and leaped toward Jennifer Orme, as she ran, bewildered and desperate, straight toward the crumbling walls. Another few seconds and anything might have happened, but, sweeping her up in his arms, he made for the open.

"Thank you," she said with surprising self-control as he set her on her feet. "The dust blinded me. I lost my head completely."

With Sulphur Riley, Jim saw to it that the others got out of the danger zone at once. They stood in a sober group a little apart, questioning one another with their eyes. The destruction had ceased, but a pall of dust would cloak the area for hours.

"I don't ever want a narrower squeak than that one was!" Dave Sprague exclaimed. And Hans Krock mourned: "I lost half-a-dozen priceless photographic plates that time—one of that very section before it fell!"

"I d-don't know about the rest of you," Balto Stubbs stuttered in his nervous excitement, "but I thought I heard a sort of dull explosion just before the c-crash!"

"What's that?" Morningstar caught him up sharply. "Are you sure it was a blast you heard?" Carlotta's warning came back to him.

"Nonsense!" Dr Birdsall interposed before Stubbs could answer. "It was the first wall crashing that he heard. Who would blow up a ruins of this nature? It's preposterous. . . . These accidents happen," he drove on, as if determined to look on the harmless side of things. "From now on we'll simply have to exercise more care.

I don't propose to send any member of the expedition home crippled or worse."

Even Stubbs was inclined to agree with him, admitting that he could not be sure about the explosion. The party returned to camp, shaken by their adventure. By the time supper was eaten they had succeeded in convincing themselves it was no more than a thrilling interlude to be retailed around the Foundation's council table in New York.

They would have been considerably interested could they have overheard a conversation between Morningstar and Sulphur on the same subject later that evening. "Them ruins tumblin' in like that was no accident, by a long shot," the lanky puncher opened up forebodingly. "Somethin' snaky's goin' on here, Jim!"

The other had already arrived at the same conclusion. "In my mind, it hooks up with that knife business. Whoever threw the knife knows plenty about this affair."

"Yo're dead right," Sulphur assented, adding: "Thing fer us to do right now is to pull up stakes an' drift—an' I mean the whole outfit! Whoever these gents are, it's mighty plain they're all done tossin' knives with notes stuck onto 'em!"

"Something in that," Jim agreed. "But Doctor Birdsall will hardly listen to any such proposal, and I believe the others would feel the same way. It looks like it's up to us, Sulphur. We'll just have to keep our eyes peeled day and night."

The following afternoon Jim found Doy Kee loitering near the water tanks when he should have been elsewhere. He ordered the Oriental away sharply. "Don't ever let me catch you here again!" he warned. He had not forgotten how closely events seemed to follow Carlotta's veiled hints made in Reno.

That day a series of inexplicable discoveries were made in the mud-walled rooms, some of them sealed, behind the section which had crashed down. In an underground kiva a few days later Dr Birdsall found a small carved Buddha. It dumfounded him and threw his companions into feverish excitement.

Doy Kee, on being questioned, had nothing whatever to contribute in the way of a solution, but later a sort of explanation turned up when Stubbs and Bill Merriam unearthed several skeletons. Bamboo-soled slippers, obviously Chinese, still clung to their feet. Even to Jim and the cowboys it became plain then that in some strange manner these Oriental remains had been superimposed on the older, authentic Indian culture of the pueblo. However it had happened, Doy Kee insisted he knew nothing about it.

"It seems incredible that the Chinese should have used a crumbling pueblo for their own burials," Jennifer remarked to Morningstar as they talked it over. "Usually they'll go to any lengths to send their dead home to be buried in the soil of China. . . . But that seems to be what has happened here."

"I've been wondering"—Jim nodded—"whether it isn't the real answer to all our difficulties. Naturally the Chinese, knowing their dead were going to be dug up, would go to some lengths to put a stop to it." Even as he spoke he was remembering certain words of Carlotta Soong's; and there was that otherwise meaningless warning received when the knife had been thrown into camp. The dynamiting of a part of the ruins, timed to endanger the lives of the Flagler party, did not in any wise conflict with this theory.

"It seems fantastic to think there are living Chinese in this wasteland," said Jennifer. "However, I shall suggest to Doctor Birdsall that we carefully rebury these bones. Then, if we really are being watched, they'll see that we intend no desecration. It may put an end to all this mystery." Jim said he hoped she was right. "As for myself," she went on, "I've been thinking of making a trip to the rimrock. I've been letting my own work go too long."

"I shouldn't if I were you," he surprised her by saying.

"But why not? Surely you don't think anything can happen to me?"

"I don't know," he said slowly. "But my suggestion is that none of us leave camp till we know exactly where we stand." Mildly as he spoke, there could be no doubt of the firmness of his position.

"I think you're taking the wrong slant, Morningstar," objected Bill Merriam, who had come up as they were talking. "Personally, I don't intend to let anything stand in the way of my going into the rimrock today."

Jim attempted to dissuade him from his plan, but without success. Merriam's faith in his ability to take care of himself in any circumstances remained unshaken. At length Jim said: "Well, if you're bound to go then I'll go with you."

They started an hour later. Although Sulphur and the other punchers had pulled away earlier that morning Jim did not question the safety of those remaining behind.

Scarcely had they got beyond sight and sound of camp when there was a flash of color in the sunlight and Doy Kee stepped from behind a boulder to confront them. As usual, his seamed, waxen yellow face told nothing.

"What are you doing out here, Doy Kee?" Jim inquired. For answer the Oriental held up a hand.

"Go back," he said. "No go 'way flom clamp."

Jim's smile concealed his immediate interest. "Don't you think we'll be quite safe in the hills, Doy Kee?"

Seeing at once how lightly they meant to take his warning, the latter seemed to gain in stature, and a scowl overspread his visage. "Go back!" he repeated authoritatively. "Doy Kee no joke. You no go limlock!" A gun suddenly appeared in his hand, its muzzle trained on them.

Bill Merriam's jaw dropped in his surprise. But Morningstar had half expected something of the sort. He had edged closer to the Chinese as he talked; the kick he let fly sent the Oriental's gun sailing through the air. Doy Kee grasped his stinging fingers and seemed to shrink, staring back at Jim stolidly, inscrutably.

"What's the idea, Doy Kee?" Jim demanded sharply. "Why are you so interested in what we do?" But he soon found that he was going to get nowhere with questions. Doy Kee went dumb. Jim could only give him up with a rueful grunt and head him back toward camp with a curt warning.

"What in the world do you suppose was behind that move?" Merriam queried as they started on.

"I don't know," Jim grunted. "But I don't intend to let it worry me any." Whatever his private thoughts were on the subject he kept them to himself.

For miles the rimrock stretched out above the pueblo, broken by lonely canyons and craggy cliffs. Merriam was an ornithologist. There was little he did not know about the desert birds, and Jim soon became interested in his work. Despite a lifetime spent in the open there was plenty to be learned from Bill.

They were high in the lonely hills, with the sun standing almost directly overhead, and were beginning to think of stopping for the lunch they had brought with them, when a distant halloo reached Jim's ears. It came from somewhere down the rugged slope. A moment later he made out Johnnie Landers, hurrying this way. Obvious excitement gripped the puncher as he rode up. "Sure had me wonderin' if I could find yuh!" he burst out.

"What's up?" Jim demanded, at a loss as to what to expect.

"Me an' Sulphur an' Hap was ridin' the hills over west," was the answer, "when we spotted three strange riders! They knowed we was watchin' 'em, for they made tracks in a hurry."

"Were they Chinese?"

"Unh-uh." Johnnie shook his head. "They was whites, Jim—range men, near's we could make out."

Morningstar was considering his line of action even while he went on with his questioning. Finally he turned to Merriam. "I don't like to do this, but if you think you can make your way back to camp all right I'll pull away and see what I can make of this business."

"Don't worry about me," Merriam answered promptly. "I'll be all right."

Taking him at his word, Jim swung into the saddle. He and Johnnie struck off across the hills at a brisk pace. "Did you spot the tracks of these men?" he asked.

Landers nodded. "Sulphur an' Hap are trailin' 'em now. We'll overhaul 'em before long."

He was not mistaken. Less than an hour later Jim sighted Sulphur waving from a ridge a mile away. They were soon there. The lantern-jawed one pointed to pony tracks on the faint trail leading into the deeper fastness of the rugged and broken Fortifications.

"There's three of 'em, Jim," he declared, "foggin' it tight as they kin go! We only seen 'em the once!"

They took up the chase without delay. The way led deeper into the desert hills. Time was lost in finding the horse tracks which petered out again and again on the bare rock. Once they thought they had lost the strangers altogether. An hour later they were pushing ahead once more. The afternoon dragged out. An hour before sunset the sign faded out in the malpais, and this time they failed to find it again.

"We've lost them for good this time," Jim said. "There's nothing for it but to turn around."

They made better time on the return, despite his decision to pick up Bill Merriam on the way. Sunset was painting the lonely ranges when they reached the spot where the ornithologist had been left. He was nowhere about, nor did an extended search through the neighboring canyons in deepening twilight afford a glimpse of him.

"He's prob'ly back in camp puttin' on the feed bag right now," Sulphur remarked.

Jim wasn't so sure, but there was no point in asking for trouble and he said nothing. They rode the last mile to camp in thickening darkness, to find the expedition's members anxiously awaiting their return.

"Where's Merriam?" Dr Birdsall asked. "He started out with you, Morningstar." The others waited for Jim's answer.

Jim wasted no time in futile inquiries. Something told him in a flash what had happened. "If he isn't here with you then he's disappeared," he said and added the circumstances of his parting with Merriam. "Of course there's the chance that he's got himself lost; that rimrock is a tricky stretch of country. But nothing can be done tonight. If he doesn't show up by tomorrow morning we'll start a search for him."

The finality of it threw these people into a state of suppressed excitement. Even they began to realize that something sinister lay behind the mysterious happenings of the past week. They talked it over at length, their voices unconsciously lowered. If they had lost a member of their party another had come to take his place, and the name of the newcomer was Dread.

Jim found himself watching Doy Kee's every

move speculatively. What did the Oriental know of Merriam's disappearance? There was nothing to be learned from that impassive yellow face and yet Jim was so engrossed that it was not until Jennifer Orme spoke to him a second time that he realized she was there.

"You seem rather worried," was what she had said.

He smiled wearily. "I told you what could be expected. I blame myself for having let Merriam leave camp at all."

Jennifer appeared little enough alarmed by the situation, however. "Bill Merriam is all right," she declared her conviction quietly. "He will return. Somehow I feel sure of it."

But Merriam had not yet returned by the following morning. Jim knew, for the first place he went on rising at dawn was to the ornithologist's tent. It was empty. He was still standing there, asking himself what the upshot of this would be, when a hoarse shout from the other side of camp disrupted the deep morning hush. Recognizing Sulphur's voice, he started that way on the double-quick. Dr Birdsall, Balto Stubbs and others appeared in their tent doors, inquiring of one another what was afoot.

Jim found Sulphur at the modest pup tent occupied by Doy Kee. The puncher looked green in this early light, and his long jaw hung slack. "Fer Gawd's sake!" he ejaculated hoarsely.

"Take a look in yere, Jim!" He indicated the tent.

Pushing him aside, Morningstar bent forward for a look. What he saw froze him with horror and surprise. It was a long moment before he dropped the flaps and straightened. Dr Birdsall hurried up.

"What is it, Morningstar?" the doctor rapped. "What have you found now?"

"It's Doy Kee," Jim told him. "He's lying in there dead! His throat has been slashed from ear to ear!"

The others soon gathered at the spot. Their faces went white as paper when they learned what had happened. They stared at one another, silenced for once.

"This ain't no surprise to me, whatever they think about it," Sulphur muttered ominously. He had joined Happy and Johnnie Landers, standing to one side. "I been expectin' somethin' of the kind fer a long time."

"Right!" Johnnie responded. "Whoever finished Doy Kee didn't make no mistake about it, an' if yuh ask me Bill Merriam got the same thing!"

If Morningstar heard the remark, standing nearby with Dr Birdsall, he gave no sign. He was staring at something which lay on the ground beside Doy Kee's twisted body and which he had not seen before. He leaned down and picked it up; a shock coursed over him as he recognized it for what it was.

It was a small jade dragon, the exact replica of the one he carried in his pocket—but this one had been broken squarely in half! For Jim that small fact bore a deep significance.

4

"Morningstar, this is incredible—a brutal murder!" Dr Birdsall's voice broke. "What is to be done about it?"

"Nothing—if you're thinking of the law," was the reply. "We don't happen to have a policeman handy, Doctor."

"But the lives of all of us may be forfeit if this is allowed to go on—murderers slipping into camp at night without leaving a trace!" He made no attempt to hide his righteous indignation. "I'm worried about Merriam too."

"I intend to start a search for him at once," Jim told him. "If he's anywhere within reach of the pueblo, and he must be, we'll find him."

"Do so." The doctor nodded curtly. "The rest of us will set out too."

"I'll have to ask you not to do that, Doctor," Jim invited. "Keep your people busy. I'll do the looking." He turned to the punchers.

"Get up the broncs, boys," he directed. "And

stick some grub in your rolls. This may prove to be a long job."

The archaeologists were drifting toward the pueblo as Jim and his men made ready to pull away. There was an air of gloom over the camp this morning; even Jennifer's smile was saddened as she nodded to Morningstar and passed on.

Once they were alone, the buckaroos were outspoken. "Jim, yuh might's well not be huntin' fer Merriam at all, fer all the good it 'll be doin' him," Sulphur declared. "After that"—he nodded toward Doy Kee's tent—"I reckon we all know what's happened to 'im!"

"You may be right," was the unemotional answer. But there was no clue to what Jim himself thought in his tone.

Swinging in the hull a moment later, they were starting away in the direction of the hills when a hail from the pueblo turned them around. Balto Stubbs was standing on a low adobe wall, waving his arms excitedly.

"More grief, dang it all!" Sulphur groaned. But Johnnie Landers was more optimistic.

"Mebby they found somethin'," he suggested, adding: "It must be mighty interestin', from the way the perfessor's takin' on."

Stubbs waved them forward urgently, and as soon as they drew near he cried: "Merriam's been found! He's here in the pueblo! They're getting him out now!"

Morningstar needed no more. Leaping from the saddle, he was soon at the spot where Dr Birdsall and the other members of the expedition were lifting Merriam, bound and gagged, up through the narrow opening in the roof of the kiva in which he had been found. He was alive and breathing, but half suffocated. They soon had him in the open. It was Jim who stripped the gag off and freed his wrists.

"Are you all right, Bill?" Dave Sprague exclaimed. Jennifer and the others waited anxiously for the response.

Merriam mumbled something incoherently and then seemed to come to himself. Looking about the circle of familiar faces, his own showed lines of strain. He sighed heavily. "I thought it was all up with me that time," he managed.

"What happened to you?" Jim demanded.

"I—I hardly know," Merriam confessed vaguely. He seemed struggling to grasp something which eluded him. "After you left me I was all right for perhaps an hour, when suddenly something struck me on the head. I think I lost consciousness then—"

"But you saw nothing or no one?"

"Not a thing. There was a period when I seemed to be carried a long ways, and at another time a voice said something to me, over and over. But what was it?" He paused, perplexed. Finally his lips parted, then: " 'Leave the dead alone. Go back.' That was it!"

47

There was a murmur of astonishment from his associates at the words.

"Was it a white man who said that to you?" Jim asked quickly.

"I don't know."

"But the voice was guttural?"

"Yes."

"Could it have been Chinese?"

Merriam appeared struck by the question. "I hadn't thought of that," he admitted; "but of course it could."

He had more to tell of his adventure, but nothing which added materially to what Jim already knew. Dr Birdsall agreed that finding him in this manner was a particularly fortunate outcome, all things considered; but he found the situation sufficiently serious to merit calling Jim aside for a private conference.

"What is your opinion of these strange occurrences, Morningstar?" he asked bluntly.

Jim considered his words carefully. "Well, let's cast up what *has* happened, Doctor. First, there was the knife that was thrown into camp. The warning attached to that was plain enough, and I'm satisfied now, after your strange discoveries in the ruins, that the knife was Chinese, as Miss Orme suggested. Later," he pursued, "we saw the three strange white men in the hills. I've asked myself a dozen times how they could hook up with what has happened, without finding the answer. But the cave-in here at the pueblo that first day seems plain-enough reading now. That brings us up to Merriam's experience and Doy Kee's murder."

"How do you explain that?" the doctor queried. "If I understand you it is your belief that the Chinese are largely responsible for everything; yet certainly they would not murder their own kind to get rid of us!"

"I'm not so sure," Jim answered slowly and proceeded: "It's just possible that Doy Kee had a task to perform, in which he failed. In such an event they would think nothing of taking his life."

"That's possible—but farfetched," said Dr Birdsall dryly.

"Not at all." Jim told how, the previous day, Doy Kee had attempted to stop Merriam and himself from going into the rimrock. He confessed that, on learning of the ornithologist's disappearance, his suspicions had leaped at once to the possibility of the cook's knowing something about it. Subsequent events seemed to indicate that Doy Kee had not. "But that doesn't mean that Merriam wasn't slugged by a gang of Chinks, who warned him and flung him into the kiva."

The doctor was impressed by this reasoning. "What course of action do you recommend?" he asked.

"I should give up this exploration immediately,"

Jim told him. "It may be one of us who'll be killed next. It's mighty plain that whoever objects to our being here will go to any lengths to gain their ends."

"I was afraid you might suggest something of the kind," said Birdsall. He shook his head. "I refuse to be frightened by any such methods, Morningstar. We'll go on with our work. It's important."

"In that case," Jim concluded, "there's nothing more to be said."

He watched the doctor move away. Birdsall was tall and spare, and there was a dignity in his bearing and his habitually severe features which Jim had always considered artificial. Now, however, he was forced to admit that there was iron under the man's polished surface. Even in the face of a real threat to the safety of them all he meant what he had said.

Balto Stubbs found occasion to accost Jim later in the morning. Quite evidently there was something on his mind.

"Doctor Birdsall declares we will go on with our work as usual," he said. "What do you think, Morningstar? Is there any particular danger in following that course?"

"Of course there's danger," Jim replied. "I told the doctor as much."

"Once he has made up his mind to anything, I fear he's a hard man to dissuade," the professor declared uneasily. "But do you really think we are being foolhardy in staying?"

"I can't say as to that." Jim was curt. "I'll do my best to keep you out of difficulties. That's all I can promise."

Stubbs didn't like the sound of this and showed it. "You understand it's not myself I'm concerned about," he explained with elaborate frankness. "It's Miss Orme I'm thinking of."

Jim looked at him. He wondered if Stubbs realized that Jennifer was less troubled by all that had happened than anyone else in the party. "I don't believe anything is likely to happen to her." It ended the conversation.

But it left him with something to think about. Unconsciously his interest in Jennifer had grown until the thought of danger to her chilled his blood and left him shocked with the realization of what she meant to him. The irony of it did not escape him; a few weeks, a month, and she would be gone from his life forever.

He cursed himself for a fool. "I'm worse than an idiot to be thinking such things," he told himself. "The sooner I get this out of my mind the better."

Johnnie Landers hailed him ten minutes later.

"Boss," said Johnnie, "your orders was that no one was to stray away from camp. The lady perfessor thinks different. I tried to stop her, but no dice. That's her movin' up the slope."

Morningstar's mouth tightened. "Thanks, Johnnie," he muttered, striding away.

He was a mile from camp before he overtook Jennifer. Her field-equipment case was slung over her shoulder. She also carried a canteen and a small rucksack. Proof enough to Morningstar that she proposed to be gone for the day.

She stopped in answer to his hail, her annoyance visible.

"Jim, do I have to go all through this again? Landers tried to stop me. Believe me, I am quite capable of taking care of myself. I am armed."

A faint smile touched Morningstar's mouth at sight of the little .22 she carried.

"I'm afraid your armament is hardly adequate, Miss Orme. Doctor Birdsall holds me responsible for the safety of the expedition. I'm sorry, but I've got to ask you to turn back."

Miss Orme tucked a rebellious strand of hair into place. "And if I refuse?"

"I don't think you will," Jim answered, distracted by a pulse that beat in her throat. She was wearing a man's shirt, open at the neck. It revealed the soft loveliness of her shoulders. He told himself she should never wear glasses; she was beautiful without them.

He knew there was earnestness and a deep sense of resolve in this girl. It showed in the proud tilt of her finely chiseled chin and her strong mouth. For the right man she held a rich store of happiness. Suddenly her mood changed.

"Why must you and the others go on treating me as a woman?" she asked. "Can't you remember that I am a scientist? This isn't my first field work. I was on the Amazon last winter. We lived on a diet of head-hunters and poisoned arrows. I came through without a scratch. I'm sure I'll be all right here. . . . After all, I had to put up quite a battle to be included in this Flagler expedition. I don't propose to sit penned up in camp and accomplish nothing."

"I know how you feel," Morningstar told her. "Maybe I'm being overcautious, but until I see what the aftermath to the killing of Doy Kee amounts to you'll have to keep out of these hills."

Jennifer Orme gazed at him with a more personal interest than she had ever shown. "Obviously," she said, a smile touching her face, "argument would be wasted on you. Suppose we compromise. Now that we have come this far, let's not waste the day completely. I have sandwiches and a bottle of coffee with me— enough for two, if you are not too hungry. After lunch you can try your hand at capturing a lizard or two for me."

"Lizards?" he queried. "You mean these chucka-wallas?"

"Lizards or chuckawallas, as you prefer," she smiled.

Morningstar often remembered that afternoon as one of the happiest of his life. But they had no sooner returned to camp than he caught the taut expectancy of the members of the expedition and even of his own men. Faces were unconsciously tense. Surface amiability had cracked, revealing the frayed nerves underneath.

Sulphur and Johnnie had dug a grave for Doy Kee on a bench below camp. Jim wondered what Carlotta Soong would think when she learned that her chef was dead. But it was barely possible, he amended thoughtfully, that she knew of it already. He had not yet satisfied himself concerning her part in the mysterious occurrences here at Pueblo Grande.

Doy Kee was buried with a simple ceremony at sunset. Dr Birdsall read a few words of the burial service, and the punchers filled in the grave with their spades.

It was a somber, thoughtful evening, despite the appetizing supper Happy Failes, their new cook, set before them. The sky turned blood red before night swam up out of the draws. The expedition turned in early, silent, depressed.

Morning was more like a return to the good cheer of sober reality. Happy's breakfast call was loud and cheery. Dr Birdsall, Stubbs, Merriam and the others rolled out briskly, looking forward to a busy day. Glancing over those gathered about the table as coffee was being poured, Morningstar noted that Jennifer was late. Perhaps she had failed to hear the summons.

Thinking only to call her, he made his way to her tent. It was exactly as usual, quiet, undisturbed, the flaps hanging closed. Jim hesitated. "Miss Orme!" he called.

There was no answer. He waited a, minute, then: "Breakfast is on the table, Miss Orme. Are you coming?"

Still no answer came. Alarm leaped alive in him, but he refused to give rein to his apprehensions, calling again, louder this time. His efforts to arouse the girl attracted the attention of the others. They turned this way, looking a question.

"What's the trouble, Morningstar?" Merriam demanded. "Anything wrong?"

Instead of answering Jim grasped the flaps of the tent, flung them aside. He stared in. He had been prepared in a manner for what he found, but, even so, a dagger of anger and remorse struck at him as he saw that the tent was empty. He stood there for a long moment as if stunned, and when he turned to the others his face was gray.

"She's gone!" he got out. "She isn't here! Her tent's empty . . . Miss Orme has disappeared!"

5

"Yo're dead right about somethin' goin' on out there in the desert, Salters; I can swear to that!" Tip Slaughter shoved his hat back and mopped his broad red brow. "About the mine, we dunno yet, but it don't sound half as crazy as it did before."

"Tell me what you've learned," Slade Salters directed with poorly concealed eagerness.

They were gathered in a dusky adobe saloon run by a Mexican at the lower end of Piute's dusty, weathered street, as had been planned two weeks ago: Salters, Slaughter, Snap Clanton and Cagle. Pablo Gonzales, who ran this place, was sprawled in the corner asleep. There was no one else to overhear their low-voiced conversation.

"We picked up the relic hunters here in town, like yuh said," Slaughter replied. "Trailed 'em out to Pueblo Grande. That wasn't no mistake, either; there's shore been plenty goin' on out there. So dang much that the whole outfit's picked up an' is on its way back right now!"

Slade's alert, dark eyes snapped with interest as Tip told all that had happened to the expedition from the time a knife had been thrown into camp with what was plainly a warning attached, through the cave-in at the pueblo, Merriam's abduction, following the pursuit of themselves and the murder of the Chinese cook. Salters followed the tale closely and at its end asked several curt questions.

"Who was it who snagged Merriam?" he queried. Tip shrugged.

"We didn't see that. But I reckon it was the Chinks."

"Were you spotted by anybody except Morningstar and his crowd?"

"Not that I know of. But there's an awful creepy feelin' about that country, Slade!" He rubbed his hands on his thighs uneasily. "Makes yuh feel like the ghost was walkin'—"

Salters brushed this aside brusquely. "Then you agree with me that my hunch was right?"

"If yuh mean there's prob'ly a mine out there somewheres—yes. Nothin' else would rile up even the Chinks so much."

Slade made no attempt to hide his satisfaction. For half an hour they talked the situation over, trying to hit on a means of definitely locating the mine. They were still at it when Salters suddenly exclaimed, lowly and forcefully: "Hold it a minute!" He was staring toward the window. The others followed suit in time to see a slowly moving hat pass by the high mud sill of the window. A moment later they saw the same thing at the other window. Tip relaxed.

"Shucks, that ain't nothin'—jest some Mex peddler or somethin'."

Salters, however, was leaving nothing to chance. Moving quietly to the door, he jerked it open and collared the man he found sitting on the doorstep. It was an old, wrinkle-faced Chinese, a basket of vegetables on his arm. Slade hauled him inside. "What's the big idea, John? What were you sitting there for?"

The old man blinked at him stolidly. "Me no sabby," he said. Salters wanted to shake him violently. Instead he threw questions in a tone of angry authority. None of them got him anywhere. Finally he gave up in disgust. "Oh hell, kick him out! We'll never get anything from him."

Snap Clanton attended to it, landing the man in the dust outside, his basket rolling. Philosophically, the Chinese picked himself and his vegetables up and shuffled away.

But Salters was scarcely satisfied. "Don't make any mistake about it: these Chinks are a slick bunch!" he warned. "That old bird may've been spying on us. I've worked for his kind too long to be fooled by anything!" He went on to explain something of the ramifications of the Wu-tai-shan Company, voicing his belief that every Chinaman in the state was secretly working in unison. What Slaughter and his companions had seen in the desert was more than enough to convince them he was right. They were still on the subject when

Bart Cagle, on watch at the window, exclaimed:

"Boys, here's Morningstar's whole outfit! They're pullin' into town now!"

The others were soon at the window. They watched the arrival of the Flagler expedition, with its many pack horses, Jim Morningstar and Dr Birdsall riding at its head. Salters' eyes blazed up at the sight.

"You were dead right, Tip!" he smiled grimly. "Sure enough, they're pullin' out, lock, stock an' barrel! This is a break for us!"

Using his eyes to some purpose at the moment, Slaughter grunted: "Hold on, where's that girl they had with 'em?"

Jennifer Orme was absent. There could be no doubt of it. Salters turned it over for a moment in his mind, but it was Snap Clanton who jerked out: "By gravy, the Chinks 've got 'er, that's what! It's why they're pullin' out!"

Unaware of interested eyes watching his every move alertly, Morningstar got the expedition to the weathered two-story Piute Hotel. There the scientists dismounted dispiritedly. Sulphur and the punchers took care of the horses, while Dave Sprague, Stubbs and Hans Krock stepped into the hotel bar. Dr Birdsall turned to Jim.

"I suppose the best thing is to see the sheriff at once, Morningstar?"

Jim nodded. "We'll go down to his office right

now." He and the doctor started that way, and Bill Merriam, looking haggard but determined, accompanied them. Jim didn't ask why. He had long since come to understand Merriam's interest in Jennifer Orme.

Huck Mulhall, the sheriff, had his office in the building that housed the jail. Jim stepped first through the door, wondering what Mulhall would suggest, but there was nobody here except a Chinese boy busy cleaning up the place.

"Where can I find Mulhall?" Jim asked.

"Shelliff no here," the Oriental pattered. "China boy hurt at Laftel-O Lanch. Shelliff back tomollow mebby."

"Then where's his deputy?"

"No dleputy," was the answer. Jim got the idea this boy was secretly anxious to get rid of them. However, there was nothing more to be got out of him. Jim and the others turned away. Dr Birdsall was frowning.

"It seems strange that this should happen just now," he remarked, as they headed for the hotel. Jim agreed.

"I can't remember seeing a Chink around the place before."

"No, no," Birdsall said impatiently. "I mean it's particularly unfortunate about the sheriff being away—"

"Doctor," Jim interposed, "I think the best thing for you and the others to do is to pull out, go back to Reno. I intend to do everything possible to bring Miss Orme back, safe and unharmed."

"But it's our duty to help," the doctor exclaimed. "Miss Orme has been with me before; she's more than just a fellow scientist to me. Anything I can do—"

"That's it," Jim said quietly. "You can't do anything. You will only be in the way."

Birdsall sighed. He was not an unreasonable man. "We'll go then. I understand there's a stage in the morning."

"You and the others may go," Bill Merriam struck in, tenseness in his voice, "but I'm staying!"

It was scarcely a surprise to Jim. He made no attempt to dissuade Merriam. "I'll see you all down at the hotel shortly," he said and turned away.

It was his intention to have a talk with Sulphur Riley, but as he headed for the livery to which the punchers had gone he noted, approaching him, the Chinese who had been at the jail. The boy came up with purpose in his manner and halted before him. It was sufficient of a surprise in itself to make Jim wary, but his eyes opened even wider, and then narrowed to slits, when the Oriental guardedly opened the fingers of one hand to reveal a small carved dragon lying on his palm. It was the exact replica of the one Jim carried.

The latter was little interested in mysteries just

61

now, however. Looking the other full in the eye, he grunted: "What?"

"You want I help you—come with me," was the answer. With superb self-assurance the speaker turned and started down the street. Jim followed, more out of grim curiosity than anything else. He knew how futile questions would be. But, convinced as he was that the Chinese were at the bottom of Jennifer's disappearance, anything interested him which led in that direction.

His guide took him to a Chinese grocery store, presided over by a fat, bland-faced sphinx. There was a brief colloquy in singsong Chinese, and then the grocer said to Morningstar: "You come."

Jim followed him to the rear of the store. A door in a dusky hall gave upon a small rear room showing the evidences of frugal living. From the rear window the view was all of sun-grayed sagebrush and distant desert ranges, as Jim was careful to learn, but even as he turned away from the window a door opened softly. He whirled sharply and then held his breath. Carlotta stood there before him.

"Why are you here?" he demanded, surprise putting an edge on his tone. In her tailored suit she was more white than Chinese.

"I've been waiting for you, Jim. Is this my welcome?"

It crossed his mind in a flash that if she had been awaiting him and knew he was coming, then she must know why he had come. "Then you and your friends *were* behind all that's happened," he said with no softening of his tone. "Carlotta— I want to know what has happened to Jennifer Orme."

Something intense flashed behind the girl's dark eyes, to be gone in a twinkling. But she could not hide from herself the sudden sharp twinge there was for her in this man's interest in another woman. It was this that kept her silent.

"I remember your warnings," Jim went on rather bitterly. "I'm afraid you were well informed. That cave-in at Pueblo Grande was no accident. Certainly that was far enough to go in your effort to protect the Chinese graves there in the ruins. But killing Doy Kee—"

"You must believe me when I say that was a mistake," Carlotta broke in calmly. "There were white men in the hills who were thought to be a part of your party. It meant that Doy Kee had failed us. I would never have gone that far, Jim—but mine is not the only voice."

Morningstar gazed at her, trying to read her secret. "Am I to gather that you are a member of some all-powerful secret society—some tong or brotherhood?" He shook his head. "It sounds incredible, and yet I can't say that it does. It's been my secret thought ever since I picked this up." He held out to her the broken pieces of the little jade figurine he had found beside Doy Kee's body.

"Obviously," he continued, "the little dragon is the secret symbol of your organization. Fail it and the token is broken. Is that it?"

There was no reading the light in Carlotta's eyes. She fingered the broken bits of jade for a moment before depositing them in front of the little joss that sat on a shelf in the corner of the room. "I gave you the little dragon as a talisman—a good-luck piece. In your case it has no other significance. You can hardly say it has failed you. As for Doy Kee, I can only repeat that his death was a mistake. He was my friend and really a great scholar; not the humble cook you took him to be." She measured Morningstar with her dark, beautiful eyes. "I am almost tempted to answer your questions," she murmured. "I know you would respect my confidence."

Their eyes held for a long moment.

"I wonder if I could," he said. "I know your hand is in many things. The very convenient absence of the sheriff, for instance."

"Nothing has happened to Sheriff Mulhall," she said without interest.

"Making away with Mulhall might be going a little too far," he said. His sarcasm was wasted on Carlotta. There was something impregnable about this girl. He felt nettled with himself, immature. In quite a different tone he said: "Who were those men on the desert—the three who were mistaken for our people?"

"They'll be discouraged," she smiled.

She made no attempt to lighten her evasion. Jim burst out: "But why? What's behind it all? Let's be done with all this mystery!"

Carlotta's eyes blazed up, dark and warm and dangerous. Unconsciously she leaned toward him in the sudden intensity of her feeling. "Jim, almost twenty years ago at Union City Dan Morningstar led an attack on the Chinese miners there—not because a white man was killed, but because a white woman—a Mexican girl—had dared to marry a Chinese. They were driven into the desert in the dead of winter: young men and old men and even women! That Mexican girl carried a baby. She saw her husband drop, wounded, unable to crawl farther. Two days later she died—out on the open desert. But the baby was saved. . . . I am that baby."

Carlotta looked at him long and inscrutably. "And you, Jim, are Dan Morningstar's son," she said almost in a whisper. "I ought to hate you, but I—I find it rather impossible." She broke off as if struggling with forces she was unable to control.

Morningstar was surprised and moved by this story of cruelty and injustice, and he could not dissemble the fact. Much of the story was not new to him. "My father died regretting his part in that affair," he said. "Hatreds were aflame in this state in those days that would shame any man.

Times have changed, thank God. Nothing like that could happen today."

"I sometimes wonder," Carlotta murmured tremulously. "I was raised and educated by my father's friends. When I was sent back East to school I was quickly made to realize what my lot was to be." Emotion shook her savagely for the moment, then abruptly let her go. "Perhaps you can understand why I refer to the Chinese as my people. I've dedicated my life to serving them."

She told him she had organized the Wu-tai-shan Company and something about its ramifications.

"We've been careful to give it the appearance of being just an importing firm," she continued. "Actually it goes much farther."

"You mean it's a tong—a secret society?" he asked.

"It's co-operative, in a way that a tong never could be—though we patterned it after the original five companies. What we own we own together. We've been satisfied to take only what white men found worthless and never asked anything but to be left to ourselves. Apparently that was too much to ask." Her tone was suddenly bitter.

"I'm beginning to understand," Jim told her. "In some mysterious way a number of Chinese have found it possible to grub a living out of this desert country to the south."

"Obviously," she admitted.

"And those graves in the Pueblo Grande—are they the graves of the people who were driven out of Union City so long ago?"

"Yes—though most of them have been returned to China."

"Then am I to understand that the disappearance of Miss Orme and all the rest of our troubles are due to the fact that we disturbed those graves?" he persisted.

Carlotta had foreseen the question and was ready for it. "Jim, you will have to accept it as the only reason," she said with unassailable dignity. "As for Miss Orme—I will take you to her. The law has no place in this matter. This must be between you and me."

A thought ran through Morningstar that brought him up short. Was this a trap? Did Carlotta intend to lead him into the same blind alley into which Jennifer had disappeared?

But there were other forces than caution at work in him. From the moment she had stepped into this room he had been conscious of the strange tug she had for him. Again he caught himself thinking how desirable she was. She liked him, that was plain. Her saying that she ought to hate him was proof enough that she did not. The charm of her manner, her warm lips, the deep mystery of her eyes, the rounded whiteness of her arms were not lost on him.

"I've got to trust her," he told himself soberly.

"There's no other way out of this." Aloud, he said: "How long will this take?"

"It may take a week."

He thought it over. A week was a long time to waste if he wasn't sure what he was doing. "Doctor Merriam has a very personal interest in anything that concerns Miss Orme," he told her. "He'll have to be consulted if the sheriff is to be kept out of this."

Carlotta's lips curved at his mentioning Merriam's interest in Jennifer Orme. "Convince him—without saying too much," she advised. "I know you will use discretion." And then, like a cry for understanding: "Jim, why are you making it so hard for me to help you?"

Morningstar moved his high shoulders restlessly. A battle went on in him. Jennifer seemed infinitely remote now. Carlotta, with her perfect oval face and the mystery and allure of an ancient race in her dark eyes, the long curve of her lips warm with the blood of her Mexican mother, her skin as smooth and flawless as ivory, affected him like some exotic perfume. He shook off its spell.

"I'll go with you," he said abruptly. "When shall we start?"

"You may come for me early in the morning," she answered, her voice soft and proud. "I will be waiting."

6

Morningstar met Bill Merriam in the street not a hundred yards from Chun Ga's store. The ornithologist nodded soberly. "I was wondering what had become of you," he said.

"Merriam," Jim gave it to him straight from the shoulder, "I'm pulling out in the morning. When I return I'll have Miss Orme with me, I hope."

Merriam's mood lifted with his surprise. Then he hesitated, obviously skeptical. "Do you mind explaining?" he queried.

Jim gave him the gist of his agreement with Carlotta, referring to her simply as a representative of the Chinese.

"Why, this is fantastic, Morningstar!" Merriam burst out at the end. "You don't honestly expect to follow out any such mad plan, do you? You'll never get Miss Orme back that way!"

"I think I will—if the sheriff is left out of the picture. If you insist on calling in the law there's no use in my starting out. It's something we must decide now."

"Leaving the sheriff out of this and letting a week pass sounds foolhardy to me," Merriam insisted. "Suppose we discuss it with Birdsall."

"We can," Jim offered, "but I would rather not. He'll be leaving in the morning. It's what you and I think about this that's important. What can Mulhall do if you call him in? Swear out a posse and go scouring the hills. That's all. I can do that. A show of force might not help Miss Orme. We want her back safe, unharmed. . . . I think I know what she means to you, Merriam. Believe me, I wouldn't be suggesting my course if I thought there was a better way."

Merriam, nerve twisted, desperate, gave in reluctantly.

"If you'll let me have a horse I'll ride for an hour or two," he said. "I've got to pull myself together."

At the barn they found Sulphur. The latter walked up the street with Jim as Merriam rode off. They were just mounting the hotel steps when a man in the act of coming out bumped into Jim accidentally. Both turned. Morningstar found himself face to face with Slade Salters!

"Howdy, Salters," he exclaimed his surprise. "I hardly expected to meet you here in Piute!"

With the suave and pleasant bearing that had helped him so often in his business Salters laughingly excused his clumsiness, adding: "Some legal work brought me down for a few days. . . . I'm sorry to hear the expedition is calling off its work at Pueblo Grande," he proceeded smoothly.

Jim nodded. "The doctor and his friends don't take to the idea very kindly. But they're starting back for Reno in the morning."

Slade's brows rose. "Not losing any time, eh? Then I'll have company on the stage to Sodaville. My work here is about cleaned up and I'm leaving tomorrow myself."

It was Jim's turn to evince surprise. He returned it with interest. "I thought you were here on Miss Soong's business," he said. "She didn't mention it, but seeing you both here in town together, I naturally supposed—"

Something crossed Salters' face which would have been difficult to define. Jim caught the question trembling on his lips, even though the attorney stopped himself before voicing it. "No, a lawyer has a good many irons in the fire," the latter passed it off with another laugh. "As a onetime cattleman you ought to know what that means!" He passed on down the steps and strolled up the street with the appearance of having nothing whatever on his mind. But Jim was not deceived. Whatever the significance of it, Slade had received a jolt which he had not been able wholly to hide.

Even Sulphur got that much. "By gravy, it set Salters back on his heels fer some reason to have yuh tell him that gal is in town!" he exclaimed, as he and Jim watched the attorney pass on up the plank sidewalk. "It's a cinch he didn't know it before yuh spoke, Jim. What yuh reckon is the meanin' of that?"

"At a glance I'd say they were working at cross purposes," Jim responded thoughtfully. "I know it doesn't make sense, but there's a big stake up there in the rimrock or the Fortifications somewhere. That's growing plainer and plainer!"

"Yeh. An' there's danger up there too," Sulphur grunted, putting a dour look on his long face. Jim shot him a look.

"You're not suggesting we pull away now, are you?"

"Hell, no," Sulphur denied stoutly.

They watched as Salters paused before the dingy office of a local lawyer, some distance down the street, and then stepped in. They would have been interested to watch his procedure once he disappeared through the door. He spent a moment with the Piute man, and when he made ready to leave it was toward the rear door that he turned. A glance at his face as he made his way along the rear of the buildings would have told that there was plenty on his mind.

Reaching Pablo Gonzales' saloon, he entered and ran lightly up the rear stairs. Tip Slaughter and his companions were lounging in an untidy bedroom overlooking the front of the building. They broke off a card game to gaze at him expectantly as he entered.

"Boys," he began harshly, "here's one for the book—the Empress is in town!"

They expressed their surprise in muttered exclamations. "Danged if she don't git around!" Snap Clanton burst out. "What 'd yuh do, Slade—run plumb into 'er?"

Salters shook his head. "I don't even know where she is. Morningstar just happened to drop the remark that he was with her."

"Morningstar, eh?" Slaughter's chilly eyes narrowed. "Why, I seen that hombre an' some Chink steppin' into this here Chun Ga's grocery store a while ago—"

"Then that's where she is," Clanton interposed. He seemed sure of the fact, but Salters gave them all a slow look.

"We've got to know definitely," he said. Clanton's broken-toothed grin flashed out.

"Ain't gittin' panicky, are yuh?" he demanded.

Slade shook a curt negative. "I've got more on my mind than that," he said flatly. "Carlotta's being here don't look so good for us. We've simply got to find out where she is and grab her." He was laying his plans, examining them, turning them over and over as he talked. "This isn't as bad as it might be at that. For one thing, if there's anything above that pueblo she'll show us where it is! But first we've got to make sure of where to find her, so you boys can get her away."

"How we goin' to do that?" Bart Cagle demanded.

"You'll have to crawl up through the brush behind Chun Ga's place and watch the windows."

They stared at him, plainly reluctant. "That won't be so good, Slade," Clanton began. "Them Chinks—"

Salters showed him a hard grin. "Don't tell me that now, Snap. You're not getting panicky, are you?" He repeated the man's own jibe of a few minutes before.

Slaughter snorted his dry amusement. "Don't worry," he said. "We'll make shore of the Empress. If we land in a jack pot doin' it it 'll be up to you to drag us out!"

There was more talk of ways and means, and then the three renegades drifted out and down the stairs to the street. Slade made no attempt to check on their activities, for it was work of a kind they were better fitted to handle than he.

It was Slaughter who took the initiative. At his direction they saddled up and rode out of town toward the south. A mile out of Piute they circled back by means of a dry wash, dismounting and leaving their ponies several hundred yards from the street. Then they crawled up through the sage, making for the rear of the Chinese store. From a safe distance they took up the watch on the grocery. But the afternoon dragged past and they saw nothing to indicate that the girl they sought was within.

Sunset drew a flaming mantle over the desert and slowly faded out. When night began to thicken Tip stood up, flipping his cigarette away.

"Might's well git goin'."

They made their way carefully through the brush in the direction of Piute's street. It was not difficult to pick out Chun Ga's grocery. There were lights in the rear windows now, but shades had been pulled down.

"Thought so," Clanton grunted disgustedly. "We'll have to bust into that place yet to find out what we wanta know."

Slaughter was not so hasty. "We'll jest keep a close watch fer a while," he muttered. "Yuh never can tell what 'll turn up."

They prowled about the place, being careful not to come too close to the chicken yards. Once Cagle stumbled over an unseen obstacle and measured his length on the ground noisily, to be sharply reprimanded by Slaughter. For a long time they saw nothing of interest. Even Tip was beginning to wonder whether their vigil would prove fruitless, when suddenly Snap grasped his arm.

"Take a squint," Clanton jerked out, keeping his voice down. "There—at that second window!"

Slaughter did as he was directed. For a moment he saw nothing. Then a shadow moved across the lighted shade, trim and small—the shadow of a woman. Cagle saw it too.

"It's her!" he exclaimed. "It can't be nobody

else. These Chinks don't have no women in this country."

Even Slaughter was satisfied that he was right. He thought a minute. "Snap, you and Bait keep a watch here," he directed then. "I'll hustle back an' tell Slade."

Turning away, he made haste in reaching the attorney in the room above Pablo Gonzales' place. Salters was waiting impatiently; he started up as Tip came in.

"Well, what about it?" he demanded.

"We've found her—she was at that Chink grocery, all right. Better get down there right off, Slade."

Salters grunted. He was soon ready to start. "What about these Chinks?" Slaughter went on, as they passed down the stairs and into outer darkness. "They goin' to give us any trouble?"

"They will if they can," was the answer.

They joined the pair in the brush behind Chun Ga's store a few minutes later. Clanton peered into the lawyer's face. "You, Slade?" he said with evident relief. "Wal, let's get this business over with."

He was only expressing the inner nervousness of them all. For ten minutes they talked in low tones, deciding just what was to be done and how. It was Salters' intention to keep himself out of sight as much as possible and return to the hotel immediately the job was done.

Clanton said: "When we've got 'er I s'pose we'll be headin' fer the pueblo, eh?"

"That's the last place in the world you're heading," Slade caught him up. And to Slaughter: "Tip, you know this country better than the rest. How far is it to that old Mormon fort on Furnace Creek?"

"Mebby eighty miles."

"Does Cache Tupper still run it?"

"Far's I know—"

Salters nodded. "Then that's where you're taking the Empress. You can handle Cache any way you have to and stay there till I come. It may be three or four days."

Tip was still thinking hard. "What 'll we be tellin' her 'bout all this?" he inquired.

"Tell her nothing," was the flat answer. "I'll do the talking when I get there."

But Slaughter was scarcely satisfied. "Slade— we're goin' up against a tough crowd in these Chinks, snatchin' their woman this way. If they get wise we won't stand a chance!"

Salters looked at him almost pityingly. "Leave it to me," he said. "I'll take care of that. I'll be going out by stage tomorrow morning," he went on, "and I'll get off at Mesquite Springs, pick up a pony and head for Horse Thief Valley. Bronc Yeager owes me his neck, and he won't forget it. He'll throw in with us. That ought to make you boys feel better about bucking the pigtails, if that's bothering you so much. I'll have to promise Bronc a cut, but it won't be much. When I get to Furnace Creek he and his crowd will be with me."

"With them to help, we ought to be able to handle anythin' that comes up." Clanton nodded approval. Salters nodded.

"We'd better. We're in this to our necks now, and we're not backing out!"

7

The sun was just lifting above the horizon, fiery red with the promise of coming heat, when Morningstar headed for Chun Ga's store the following morning.

The place was closed and silent at this hour. But he was not surprised. Passing through a vacant lot, he made for the rear of the building. Here, too, the shades were drawn and there was no sign of life. Only when his brisk knock failed to bring any response did he take alarm. He knocked again, louder. Still there was no answer.

Lips closed, tightening to a grim line, he ran his eye over the building, then tried the door handle. To his surprise it turned easily. Shoving the door open, he stepped in. "Chun Ga!" he called. "Carlotta! Are you here?"

Only silence answered him.

He tried the first hall door he came to and found that it gave upon the room in which he had met Carlotta the day before. It was empty now. He didn't bother to look around. Next he tried a bedroom. It showed signs of recent occupancy, though it was tenantless now; the faint traces of a familiar perfume told him Carlotta had used this room. Certain he had been duped, he flung into the hall and tried the remaining door. It resisted momentarily, then sprang open with a jerk. Jim halted on the threshold.

This time his search was rewarded. There could be no mistaking that stout bulk lying on the tousled bed. It was Chun Ga. But as Jim stared he divined that something was wrong. The next moment he made sure. Stripping back the single blanket, he saw that the grocer was not asleep, but bound and gagged!

It was the work of only a moment to strip off the gag and start working on the Oriental's bonds. Chun Ga grunted and rolled his eyes. Seeing him conscious, Jim flung hasty words at him: "What happened, Chun Ga? Where's Carlotta?"

"She gone," was the answer, after a maddeningly deliberate pause. "Last night, evelything all light. Moy Quai happy. I go bed, go 'sleep. White mens come—hit Chun Ga—knock outa bed—tie up—take missy."

"White men, you say?" Jim rasped. "Did you recognize any of them?" And at Chun Ga's headshake: "How many of them were there then?"

Again that massive, fatalistic shrug. "Mebby thlee, fo'."

While Jim went on with his questions his mind was already busy with what he had learned. Chun Ga either couldn't, or wouldn't, add anything material to it, but that was scarcely needed. The image of one man loomed large in Jim's suspicions now, and that man was Slade Salters.

Jim remembered back to the night of the dinner in Carlotta's apartment in Reno. Even then he had felt the wire-thin thread of tension and antagonism between the girl and her attorney. It had all started over the remarks of Clay Masters, about the possibility of an unrecorded gold mine somewhere in the desert. Then Salters had come down here to Piute—without even guessing that Carlotta was here also.

"What an ass I was to tell him!" he muttered. "I wanted to draw him out—but it wasn't worth this."

Swinging into the saddle, he kicked his bronc in motion and started for the hotel, where he had last seen Salters. Before he was halfway there a voice hailed him and he whirled to see Bill Merriam.

"I thought you were well on your way by now, Morningstar."

Jim jerked a curt negative. "My plans have been knocked higher than a kite!" he flung over

80

his shoulder as he hurried on to the hotel. "Tell you later!"

Merriam's jaw dropped. "Well I'll be damned!" he cried, following him on the run.

As for Jim, he was asking himself if he would find Salters in Piute this morning or whether the attorney had slipped away already. In the latter event, it would clinch the matter of Slade's guilt but wouldn't be much help otherwise. In fact it would only further complicate affairs already too complicated.

To his surprise, when he drew in his bronc before the hotel and glanced through the window, he saw Salters serenely eating his breakfast in the dining room. Swinging to the ground, Jim made for the door, and, a moment later, stood at the lawyer's table.

Slade glanced up with pretended surprise. "Why, good morning—" he began. Jim cut him off with a flat challenge that made Bill Merriam, standing behind him in the doorway, jump with amazement.

"Salters, what have you done with Carlotta Soong?"

Slade started to rise from his chair, his expression altering, then sank back. "Done with Miss Soong?" he echoed. "I don't know what you mean. What has happened to her?"

"She's disappeared," Jim snapped. "I think you know plenty about it!"

Something deadly flickered for an instant in Slade's dark eyes. Then he laughed. "Why, this is preposterous!" he exclaimed. "If anything has happened to her I know nothing of it. Why should I? I've been her lawyer for years, Morningstar." He grew thoughtful. "I'll admit I don't know too much about this Wu-tai-shan Company— her Chinese firm. Perhaps they spirited her away." He refused to grow excited, lifting an inquiring glance. "What do you think happened?"

He sounded so plausible that Jim hesitated. Had he leaped to too hasty a conclusion? He recalled Carlotta's saying that where the policy of the Chinese was concerned hers was not the only word. Yet she had promised to lead him to Jennifer. Had her people taken decisive steps to prevent her? He had only Chun Ga's word that white men had carried her off.

"I'm not thinking about this, Salters—I know," was Jim's slow answer.

Salters brushed this aside, insisting on an account of what had happened. Jim accommodated him. Slade turned it over, his eyes darting absently. Suddenly he said:

"It's a strange business, I'll grant. But why were *you* down to that Chink store so early in the morning? Did Miss Soong by any chance offer to take you to Miss Orme?"

The shrewdness of it brought Jim up short. Salters had learned the details about Jennifer's disappearance from Dr Birdsall and the others. Plainly he had put two and two together as to what had become of her.

"If her people objected why should Carlotta offer to help me?" There was a deliberate evasion in Jim's query. It was almost as though he, and not Salters, were on the defensive. And yet his suspicions of this man were by no means allayed. "I'm waiting to hear what you propose to do about this," he continued. "You've been her attorney for a long time. You might be expected to show a little concern over her disappearance."

Slade pretended indignation, but managed a laugh. "I told you I've finished my work here. I'm taking the stage this morning for Sodaville. . . . I'm going on to Reno. . . . Of course I'll help the authorities any way I can," he concluded.

Morningstar stared him to silence. "Salters, if this was all I knew about you it would be enough to give me your number. You're a first-class rat. I'll prove that to you one of these days." With a shrug of contempt he turned on his heel and walked out.

Merriam joined him in the lobby and they stepped out to the hotel veranda. It was Bill who spoke first. "This can't go on, Morningstar!" he burst out forcefully. "I've got to know that something is being done about Miss Orme. I'm going to the sheriff the minute he returns and demand immediate action!"

Jim rolled and lit a smoke before he answered. "I can hardly ask you to do otherwise now. Meanwhile, I'll watch every move Salters makes."

"But if he's going to Reno—" Bill started to argue.

"He *says* he's going there," Jim interposed. "I think he's lying. I'm going to do a little checking up on him. Come along. We'll go hunt up the boys."

Sulphur and Johnnie and Hap were not at the livery but were found in a saloon near by. Jim called the lanky Irishman aside. "Sulphur, didn't you tell me you knew the driver of the Sodaville stage?" he asked.

"Sep Williams? Wal, I should smile," Riley responded, without a trace of expression crossing his face. "What's that old juniper been doin' now?"

Jim lost no time in acquainting him with what was wanted. "I'll see to it," Sulphur promised, taking the money Morningstar handed him. A moment later he went off in search of Williams.

He was back in twenty minutes. "It's okay," he assured Jim. "I gave Sep the money, an' he says he'll send a messenger back right off if Salters leaves the stage this side of Sodaville. If he don't Williams promises he'll make sure Slade gits on the train fer Reno an' let yuh know accordin'."

"Good." Jim was more than satisfied. He turned to Merriam. "If you've got any good-bys to say to your friends you'd better say them quick, if you're going to string along with me this morning." He

84

instructed Sulphur to get Johnnie and Happy Failes and bring them to Chun Ga's store at once.

Merriam accompanied Jim up the street. They could see the stage standing before the hotel. It was getting ready to leave. Dr Birdsall and the others were aboard, their belongings piled about them. Merriam said good-by to them.

"I hope you'll find Miss Orme speedily, Morningstar," Dr Birdsall called down soberly. "Let me know the minute you learn anything. I'll be waiting anxiously for news."

Jim nodded. There was no point in mentioning Carlotta. Slade Salters sat in a corner of the stage, rolling a cigar over in his lips. The look he gave Morningstar was almost amused.

Sep Williams, a grizzled, salty old-timer, climbed to the box and picked up the reins. The stage horses knew all the signs. Even as Sep reached for his long black snake they started up. With a rattle of wheels the stage started on the long and dusty trip across the desert to Sodaville.

Jim was standing there, thinking of Salters' smooth inscrutability, when through the dust came riding a black-bearded, heavy-set man on a bay gelding. Jim recognized Huck Mulhall.

The sheriff had already spotted him, for he came forward directly and stepped to the ground at once. "I want to talk to yuh, Morningstar," he said.

"What about?" Jim countered, not bothering to hide his surprise.

"Dave Brant stopped me as I rode past his place half an hour ago," Mulhall enlightened him. "He had an excited Chink there—a friend of his cook. It was Chun Ga, who runs a little grocery here. I managed to get out of him that a girl was abducted from his place last night. It seems you visited her yesterday. What do yuh know about this?"

"I don't know a thing, Mulhall, beyond what Chun Ga told me," Jim answered.

"Well!" the lawman grunted. "That don't sound right. If yo're goin' to take that slant I'll hold yuh."

"You don't mean you're arresting me?" Morningstar questioned, alarmed only at the threat of being delayed.

"That's as good a name fer it as any," Mulhall said unemotionally.

"But you can't do that!" Merriam protested angrily. "I'll tell you why he saw Miss Soong. She was going to help us find Jennifer Orme."

Jim shook his head and prepared himself for what was to follow.

"Jest who is she?" the sheriff demanded suspiciously.

There was nothing to be done but explain. Mulhall's face reddened as he listened, and at the end he exploded with a fine show of indignation.

"Why wasn't my office notified about this?" he demanded. "Believe me, I'm holdin' the both of yuh now!"

8

Jim found time for sober reflection as he and Bill Merriam accompanied Mulhall toward the latter's office in the jail. Both Jennifer and Carlotta he knew to be in real danger; either might be dead. As for Carlotta, if emissaries of her own people had her she would be in even graver peril than if some of Slade Salters' thugs had abducted her.

He had not forgotten his promise to the girl that he would keep the law out of this. But surely events had changed that now. If there was any help to be got from the sheriff for Carlotta's own good he ought to enlist it.

When they stepped into Mulhall's office Jim had made up his mind definitely. "You needn't bother to lock us up, Sheriff," he said as the latter turned to him. "I'm as anxious to get this business ironed out as you are."

"That's better," was the gruff response. "Yuh just give me the whole story, Morningstar."

That was precisely what Jim did, starting with the Feast of the Lanterns' dinner in Reno, when he had first met Carlotta, and continuing on through all that had happened to the Flagler expedition at Pueblo Grande. Next, with Carlotta's sudden disappearance, followed his inevitable suspicions of Slade Salters and the reasons for them. Nor did he omit his arrangement with Sep Williams, the stage driver, for keeping a watch on the attorney. Mulhall listened to all this attentively, tugging at his beard thoughtfully. At the end he nodded.

"I didn't think yuh could tell a story I'd be willin' to believe," he said frankly. "But yuh have. An' since yuh put all yore cards on the table I'm willin' to help yuh. I want to see both of those girls back, safe an' unharmed. But I reckon yo're right 'bout the best way of goin' at it, Morningstar. If we can find Carlotta Soong, locatin' Miss Orme 'll be considerably simplified—"

He broke off, frowning, as three men stepped in the door in ominous quiet and without so much as a by-your-leave. Jim glanced up. It was Sulphur Riley and his companions.

"What's the meanin' of this, Sheriff?" Sulphur drawled with dangerous calm. "Don't tell me yo're holdin' my friend Jim here—"

"It's all right, Sulphur," the latter broke in with a grin. "I've told Mulhall everything. We're pulling together the rest of the way." He saw the expressions of relief which washed over the punchers' faces at his words and knew the lengths to which they would have gone without question, had it been necessary to extricate him from some difficulty.

Mulhall scrutinized Sulphur and Johnnie and Happy Failes individually and thoroughly, as though sizing them up. What he saw must have satisfied him. "Yo're workin' for Mornin'star, ain't yuh? Better get ready to ride, because we're headin' out right away."

"Wal, climb onto yore bronc then, an' we'll go," was Sulphur's way of telling him there would be no delay on his account. Mulhall grunted and scraped to his feet.

"Got to get me some deputies an' swear 'em in," he said to Jim. "It won't take me fifteen minutes, if I can locate the men I want."

He was as good as his word, appearing well within the allotted time with four mounted and capable-looking men. Meanwhile Jim, Merriam and the others had moved down to Chun Ga's grocery. They were covering the ground in the rear with great care when the sheriff arrived.

"Find anythin'?" he demanded.

"Some broncs were held over here in the dry wash," Jim assented, "and it's pretty plain from the boot tracks that their riders were interested in the store. The yard's beaten too hard to learn anything there. It's my guess that Miss Soong went whichever way those ponies were headed."

Mulhall went over the ground and nodded. "Morningstar, I'll swear you an' yore friends in before we get started."

"Wait a second," Jim said. "One of us has got to

89

remain here in town, in case a message comes from Sep Williams." He turned to Bill Merriam. "I don't like to do this, Merriam, but somebody's got to stay behind."

Bill wanted to protest, but he saw the sense of it. "If I'm staying don't waste time talkin' about it!" He grinned then to show there was no hard feeling in his disappointment at being left in Piute.

There was some talk of how he was going to find them in case of need. That settled, they swung into the saddle.

Barren hills rose to the north of Piute. The trail followed by the posse threaded them interminably. Mulhall, who knew this country well, squinted ahead from time to time. Plainly there was something on his mind.

"They're makin' fer lava country up here a piece," he said at last. "Reckon we'll have trouble there." He did not say that they stood an excellent chance of losing the abductors altogether, but the possibility hung in the air after he had ceased speaking.

He was not mistaken in what he said. An hour later the sign of the horses they pursued faded out in the volcanic rubble. Fifty yards and there was not even the faint scratch of an iron-shod hoof to help them.

Sulphur was the best tracker in the posse. It was half an hour before he found any sign, and then it was only to find a broken stalk of fireweed. It was enough for him. Given the direction, he ranged far out and presently hailed the others forward with the information that he had picked up the trail again.

Now the going was slower. Evening found them in a barren, desolate country of broken ledges. Mulhall studied the sun and said: "We'll make dry camp here. There's no tank within half a day's ride of us—an' I'd hate to shove a bronc over this stuff in the dark. He'd bust a leg before yuh got half a mile."

In the first light of morning they were on their way once more.

They found the trail more difficult to hold than on the previous day. Time after time the tracks were lost, and precious hours were wasted in finding them. In this rocky, utterly treeless inferno the power and weight of the desert made itself felt. For the first time Jim began to wonder whether they would succeed in overtaking Carlotta's captors.

They had made sure of an unmistakable trail behind themselves, and so it was no surprise when Merriam caught up with them late in the afternoon. As Jim had anticipated, Sep Williams' messenger had reached Piute with word of Slade Salters' movements.

"Salters got off the stage at Mesquite Springs and headed north into the desert," Bill announced. Morningstar and Mulhall exchanged glances at the information. The former nodded.

"So I was right," he said tersely. "I don't know where Salters himself is heading, but it's plain enough that some of his renegades have got Carlotta!"

Sunset found them even deeper in the forbidding desolation of the great Amargosa Desert. The trail of the abducted girl had taken them miles from the Indian pueblo whose secret Salters evidently planned to drag from her, but neither Morningstar nor Mulhall was surprised. "He knows that might be the first place we would look for Carlotta," Jim said. "He's taking her away somewhere till things quiet down. The question is"—his brows knit thoughtfully—"where?"

There was no sure answer. They could only push on, hoping that time would allay the precautions of the men they sought. But, as Johnnie Landers pointed out, something had to break mighty soon. Their water was almost gone, likewise their food.

"Wal, we should reach Coffin Spring in a mile er so," Mulhall announced. "I've always found water there. That 'll carry us over tomorrow."

But when they located Coffin Spring, just as the afterglow was fading from the lavender-tinted sky, they found, to their chagrin, that it was dry. Mulhall said there was no other water that he knew of within thirty or forty miles.

It was a sober bunch of men who camped beside

the dry spring that night. Such water as they had was used sparingly, and even so the morrow promised early difficulties. In the morning their first move was to consider the situation.

"Salters' men must have known what they were up against and prepared themselves to meet it," Jim said. "But that doesn't help us in the slightest. Just where do we look for water from here, Mulhall?"

"Wal, there's Iron Tanks, thirty miles or so west of here," was the answer. "The water there's rank stuff—if there is any. An' then there's Skull River. It's nothin' but a pothole. That's as far or farther to the northeast." He shook his head. "I dunno which I'd say was the surest bet."

"We've got to have water," Jim said soberly. "The best thing is to divide our forces and make sure of it. We can arrange to meet somewhere by evening. At least one party is almost certain to find water."

It was so decided. A rendezvous was named for that night and they set out, Mulhall taking his deputies with him. Merriam, Sulphur, Happy and Johnnie Landers going with Jim. It was to Iron Tanks that the latter had elected to go. Mulhall's directions had been so hazy that considerable difficulty was experienced in locating the place, and then only to find it dry, as Coffin Spring had been. There was no time to hunt for some unknown tank. They had all they could do for that day to reach the designated rendezvous. To Jim's chagrin, Mulhall had been no more successful in finding water than he.

"We've either got to find water in a hurry or turn back," Jim declared grimly. "It may already be too late for us to reach Piute. Where's the nearest certain water from here, Mulhall?" He found it hard to keep a sharp impatience out of his tone, for the sheriff's "information," well meaning though it might be, had already been the cause of their losing an entire day.

"Wal, there's nothin' sure this side of Furnace Creek. Mebby one day's ride, an' mebby two."

"What do you mean?" Jim demanded.

"There's always water in the creek," was the answer, "but no tellin' how far down it's flowin' this time o' year. There may be plenty in the low spots as far east as the Vermilion Buttes, or we may have to ride clear to the headwaters, around Tupper's old Mormon fort."

They talked it over. It was decided to split once more in the morning, with plans to meet at evening of the second day somewhere near the head of Furnace Creek.

They started at three in the morning, to take advantage of the dawn coolness, and yet it proved to be the hardest day Jim had ever put in on the desert. Nothing but the white glare of sand, the red of crumbling ledges met them. A scorching wind whipped up at noon, to strengthen into a sandstorm. The horses had grown so weak that in places they had to dismount and lead them. Catching Jim's eye, Sulphur, hardened old campaigner that he was, shook his head grimly.

"We can't stand much more uh this," he declared.

By midafternoon they reached what was clearly the bed of Furnace Creek. It was dry. No digging in the sand brought any slightest trace of moisture to light. Yet Jim was visibly cheered.

"All we've got to do is follow the creek up," he told the others. "We can't miss it!"

But close of day found them as far from relief as ever. Johnnie and Hap Failes were for pushing on steadily, but Jim said no. "We'll stop for a rest," he declared. "We're only a few hours from water. We're all right now. Sometime tomorrow we'll go back and pick up the trail."

His tone conveyed a confidence he did not feel, for it would have been impossible to overlook the fact that time was passing, putting a wider gap between them and Carlotta. One aspect of the case persisted in his mind. At last he voiced it.

"If this country is tough on us it's just as tough on the men we're hunting. As for a woman—she couldn't stand it. And that bunch is going to be careful of that girl. I believe they've long since reached the place they were heading for—some place where food and water were sure."

"What about the Mormon fort that Mulhall was

talking about?" Merriam asked. "It's a chance."

"They could be holed up there!" Jim exclaimed. And then, with growing conviction: "Where could they find a better place? Boys!" he cried, "when we get our canteens full we're going to Mormon Fort!"

Night was falling when, without warning, there was a rattle of hoofs. A number of riders drew near in the soft darkness. At first Jim thought it was Mulhall and his deputies returning. He stood up. But it was not Mulhall, as he learned when the newcomers closed in in such a manner as to suggest a capture. A moment later the leader swung down and approached the fire. Jim stared. It was Quan Goon, the Chinese he had seen at Carlotta's party in Reno. He had a gun in his hands.

"Hello, Quan," Jim exclaimed, with a heartiness he was far from feeling. "How does it happen that you're here?"

The Oriental, fiercer of visage than ever, did not deign to answer. He glanced about, taking everything in. "Where is Moy Quai?" he demanded bluntly. "Miss Soong," he added for Morningstar's benefit. There was no trace of pidgin in his speech.

"I don't know, Quan. That's what we're trying to find out. That's why we are here."

Quan Goon absorbed the statement stolidly. Plainly he was not inclined to believe it. Jim shot a warning glance at Sulphur, who started to get to his feet, bristling and incensed at the look of things. The long-faced one subsided grudgingly. Quan Goon said stubbornly:

"We thing you took Moy Quai. What have you done with her?"

Jim shook his head. "You've got it all wrong, Quan. Carlotta was kidnaped all right, but not by me. Would this convince you?" He held out the little jade dragon. Quan Goon stared his surprise.

"She gave you this?"

Morningstar nodded.

"As a matter of fact," he proceeded to press his advantage, "I'm practically certain that Salters, her lawyer, is responsible for her disappearance." He told why he thought so and how he had made sure of Slade's connection with what had happened. Quan Goon heard him out and then growled: "Where will you look for Moy Quai?"

Jim told him about Mormon Fort, far up Furnace Creek.

Quan Goon squared his powerful shoulders. "We'll go there now."

"But what about the sheriff?" Jim queried. "We were supposed to meet his party. They need water, too, desperately. We can't forget about them!"

The Oriental jerked himself erect, suspicion and rage racing through him. "Didn't you promise Moy Quai to say no word to the sheriff?"

Jim explained how Mulhall had learned of Carlotta's disappearance and had promptly declared himself in on the search. Quan Goon scowled. Clearly he wanted nothing to do with the law.

Morningstar briefly considered the horsemen who ringed them in. He exchanged a glance with Merriam. He was not deceiving himself about these Chinese. He knew he was not dealing with the humble John Chinaman of the laundry counter now. These men were lean, hard-fighting men, as much at home on a horse as an Apache, and likely to be as ruthless if opposed.

"The sheriff will have to take care of himself," Quan Goon announced shortly. "We have water and food. You will ride with us."

"That suits me," Jim told him. "Pick up your saddles, boys," he said to Sulphur and the others.

"Wait!" Quan Goon broke in. "Put your guns on the ground before you go near the horses."

"What?" Jim demanded furiously. "Are we prisoners?"

"Hostages," Quan Goon answered sullenly. "No harm will come to you if we find Moy Quai."

9

For upwards of twenty years the backwaters of pioneer life had swirled about the old Mormon fort on Furnace Creek. It had seen Indian fights savage as the bleak desert in which it stood;

succored settlers on their way across the Sierras to California; become a last outpost of the strange religious sect which had taken root in Utah. It still bore the marks of those times.

Of late years the fort had been little more than a trading post, presided over by grizzled old Cache Tupper. But it still remained well-nigh impregnable, when sufficiently manned, with its stout adobe stockade and its fortificationlike buildings. Due to these things, as well as its extreme isolation, more than once Mormon Fort had been pressed into service as an outlaw rendezvous and hide-out.

Certainly it had a forbidding aspect under the cold, dead light of a late moon as Slade Salters emerged from the trade room and looked about. Cache Tupper was with him, a twisted, sly, evil-looking old man with an oily manner. In the compound Tupper halted and jabbed an insinuating thumb in the direction of a small building standing by itself in one corner of the stockade enclosure.

"Over there," he said. "That's where they put 'er."

Without replying, Salters went on toward the building, his tall straight figure cutting its brisk shadow pattern on the ground. He halted before the stout plank door and rapped smartly. After a moment the door was opened guardedly from within. Bart Cagle's suspicious visage appeared.

"Howdy, Slade," he nodded with obvious relief.

"Yuh got here finally, eh? I heard you an' Bronc's crowd ride in."

Salters' nod was curt. "I understand you've got the girl here. You can leave us for a while," he said sharply. "I want to be alone with her."

There was an evil suggestion in the glint of Cagle's eyes as he grinned acknowledgment. But all he said was: "Okay, Slade."

Slade watched till he was sure Cagle was on his way to join the others, where they were drinking together in the main building of the post. Then he stepped inside and closed the door. A crude oil lamp was burning within. In its glow Salters made out Carlotta, sitting upright in a chair, her hands bound behind its back. There was a fiery flash in her eyes as she met his regard, which he hastened to forestall.

"What, tied up?" he exclaimed with concern. "They dared do that to you? By God, I'll—"

"Never mind all that," she cut him off coldly. "You needn't pretend anything, Slade. It was you who did this to me!"

For a moment he stood looking down on her, thinking how beautiful she was in anger, even in these sordid surroundings. Then he nodded slowly, moving around behind her chair to release her hands.

"That's right," he confessed as he worked. "And I gave those fools strict orders to be gentle with you! If they think they can handle you this way and get away with it I'll soon teach them different!" His tone suggested quite convincingly that his own indignation was bubbling just beneath the surface.

"But why?" she insisted, forcing all fury and loathing and suspicion out of her voice. "Why did you have to do anything to me?"

"For your own good, Carlotta," he assured her gravely as he got the last bond loosened and she got up from the chair to chafe her bruised wrists tenderly. "You had to be brought to your senses in some way. Don't you understand," he went on with the air of a displeased mentor, "that you can't go on doing such things as killing men, and keeping Miss Orme prisoner and the like, without serious consequences? I've been your attorney for a long time; I don't propose to wait until you land yourself in a position where I'll be utterly unable to help you. It must be growing clearer and clearer even to yourself that you've kept me in the dark too long about what's going on. Don't you realize that the Wu-tai-shan Company cares nothing whatever about you as an individual; it is only their own interests that concern them, and so long as you are obedient they will ask things of you which should never be asked of anyone?"

He was watching her eyes and stopped when he saw the warning signal there. But he went on at once: "However, that's all in the past now. But I insist that you simply haven't sufficient confidence in the man in whom you should have every confidence. If you had only told me long ago what these mysterious maneuvers are about you would not be here now."

Slade paused on a flat note of waiting, as though he had delivered an ultimatum. Plainly he expected her to speak. But Carlotta only went on moving up and down to restore the circulation in cramped limbs and glancing musingly first at Salters' face and then at the oil lamp. When she spoke at last it was almost with composure.

"I'm sorry if I appear that way to you, Slade. But I can tell you nothing more than you already know."

"I see." He looked serious, pursing his lips in sober thought. She listened quietly while he went on, marshaling his reasons why she could not afford silence any longer. For a quarter of an hour she remained so unmoved that at last he burst out harshly:

"Carlotta, there's something in the rimrock above Pueblo Grande which is making you all do these desperate and foolhardy things! You must either take me there or tell me about it! Don't you see that you are endangering yourself needlessly by this absurd mystery? Good heavens! You don't think *I* am interested in whatever it is that's up there, do you?" He put all the appeal of which he was capable into the words.

Carlotta faced him calmly.

"I'm sorry," she repeated in a tone of unshaken resolution. "I can't take you anywhere or tell you anything. There's no use of your asking again."

Standing there, staring at her, Salters appeared to undergo a profound change. He hardened, ruthlessness and cruel purpose coming out in his face.

"You're making a mistake, Empress," he said thinly, throwing in her face the sardonic epithet by which she was known. "A big one! All your wriggling and squirming on the pin only proves that there's a mighty big stake behind this game. Well"—a hard grin wreathed his lips—"I'll find out yet what it is. In fact, I'm pretty certain I already know! And you'll confirm me before we get through," he nodded at her grimly.

"You have already confirmed my own opinion of you," she flashed, giving him a look of hatred. "I thought you were trying to worm something out of me for your own purpose. I'm only a woman, you were thinking; it would be easy to twist me around your finger, get what you want. . . . Well, you will not find it as easy as you supposed, Slade." She had perfect command of herself now. "I warn you, it is yourself who are making a great mistake. But it will not be long before you discover that."

Temper boiled up in Salters, and a vein in his temple throbbed. He would have retorted fiercely, even laid hands on her in the heat of his frustration, but at the moment someone banged on the door and called out urgently.

"What is it?" Slade demanded savagely.

"It's Snap!" cried the man outside. "Open up, Salters! There's trouble brewin'!"

Slade had the door open almost before he had ceased speaking. "All right, what is it?" he demanded.

"Me an' one of Bronc's boys was takin' a little *pasear* around the hills, when we was fired on." The words tumbled from Clanton's lips. "It was Huck Mulhall—the sheriff! There was four or five men with him! We give 'em the slip, but they're comin'! They'll be here in half an hour— mebby less!"

Salters pulled himself together swiftly, seeming to forget Carlotta's existence.

"Mulhall, eh?" he muttered. "We'll take care of that in a hurry!" He whirled on Snap. "Tell the boys to get ready to ride—and send Cagle over here again. We've got to leave somebody on guard while we're gone!"

Snap started away running. Almost before he was beyond earshot Slade wheeled toward Carlotta. "Sit down in that chair!" he rasped. "I'm tying you up again whether you like it or not!"

Carlotta caught back the stinging retort which trembled on her tongue. There could be no point in taunting Salters while he was in this mood.

When Bart Cagle made his appearance the girl

104

was once more securely bound. "Keep an eye on her," Slade directed the renegade sharply. "I don't want you to stir a step away from here while the rest of us are gone!"

"Okay, Slade."

Stepping outside, Salters waited only long enough to hear the bar dropped in place inside the door. Then he hastened toward the post building. Men were busy there, tossing saddles aboard their ponies, cinching up. Bronc Yeager, a rugged, granite-faced man with the stamp of the confirmed outcast on him, was waiting with the bridle of Slade's horse in his grasp.

"Let's get goin'," he ground out. "I got an account to settle with Mulhall anyway. Out here in the middle of hell is a good place to do it!"

Snap Clanton took the lead as they poured out of the stockade gate. "Mulhall's follerin' the ridge along the creek," he declared. "That's where we'll meet 'em."

They turned down the creek bed, dry at this point, and soon were putting the ponies up the rocky ridge which Clanton had indicated. Scarcely had they reached its crest, half a mile from the fort, when a warning cry rang out, and a moment later a rifle blazed at them from the cover of the rocks.

Salters turned in the saddle. "They're holed up over there in the rocks!" he whipped out. He flung a slug in that direction. But it was Bronc

Yeager who took command, accustomed as he was to skirmishing of this kind. Under his direction Slade's men and his own owlhoots spread out and drew a net about the patch of rocks from which the enemy's fire came. It swelled in volume as the issue at stake became plain, for Mulhall and his men were in desperate case. Outnumbered and suffering from lack of water, and even of food, they found no choice but to go on the defensive when they found themselves pitted against this overwhelming superior force.

A mile distant, on the way up Furnace Creek, Jim Morningstar and the others heard the heavy firing. Quan Goon and the other Chinese cocked wary ears toward the ridge from whence the sound came but showed no inclination to investigate.

"I told you what the situation was—and I was right!" Jim exclaimed to the leader. "Mulhall has clashed with Salters' outfit! We ought to get over there and give him a hand!"

Sulphur and the cowboys saw it the same way, but for once they hesitated, looking to their captors. Quan Goon listened intently for a moment and then shook his head.

"We must find Moy Quai," he announced inflexibly. A wild cry from him swept them on.

Jim was anxious to do what he could to relieve Mulhall: it was plain from the sound of the firing that the sheriff was outnumbered; but, at the same time, Jim was driven as strongly as Quan

Goon to learn whether Mormon Fort was the hiding place that had been chosen for Carlotta. In the hope that the girl might be located and freed without further loss of time he anxiously hurried up the creek with the others.

"Better hand over our guns, Quan," he told the Oriental flatly. "We won't be of much use to you without them."

Quan Goon stabbed him with a suspicious glance but nodded. "You can have your guns. Do not forget that every move you make will be watched!"

The waning moon was throwing long black shadows when they rode out on the little flat which accommodated the fort. There was no sign of life about the place. The gate was closed. They made straight for it, and it was Jim who hauled himself up out of the saddle by holding onto its top stakes. There was a flash and a bang from within, and a slug whistled past his head.

"Give me a hand here!" he flung at Sulphur.

Together they managed to reach the top of the gate. Jim dropped inside. Even as he was loosening the bars Sulphur fired at someone among the buildings.

"Git out of here!" a harsh voice yelled. "Pull out, or I'll blast yuh down!" It was Cache Tupper. He held a rifle in his trembling hands, but it was plain the weapon was more of a bluff than anything, for his aim was poor.

Jim got the last bar out and shoved the gates wide. The punchers and Quan Goon's Chinese came through with a rush. If they had expected a sharp resistance they were mistaken. Sulphur took a last snap shot at Tupper, who howled his terror and took to his heels, the rifle flying. Merriam grabbed it up.

Dismounting, the men quickly spread through the post in search of Carlotta. They left no spot unexplored. Jim was just coming out of the trade room, when a shout from another part of the compound attracted his attention. He recognized Johnnie Landers' voice. In no time he was running that way.

Johnnie was plastered against the wall of a little outbuilding, just at one side of the door.

"What is it?" Jim demanded.

"Don't git in front of that door!" Landers warned. "Some hombre's in there with a gun, an' he's drillin' holes with it!"

It was enough for Jim. He thought he understood the situation. Carlotta had been found nowhere else. If she was at Mormon Fort at all then she was here. Evidently one of Salters' renegades had been left behind to stand guard. Jim said:

"Have you tried that door?"

"No!" Johnnie jerked out. "An' if yuh ain't a dang fool yuh won't do it neither!"

Jim made for the door without a second's pause. The planks resisted his first kick, and his second.

Bullets ripped through them, perilously close.

"Lend a hand here!" he rasped as Sulphur came running up. Together they put their shoulders to the door and heaved. It gave suddenly, with the bursting of the bar; they were catapulted into the little room, almost losing their balance. It was all that saved them.

"Look out, Jim!" Morningstar heard Carlotta's frightened cry. "He'll kill you!"

Jim threw himself sidewise just as Cagle fired. The slug whined past his face. Bart attempted to shoot again. Before he could do so Sulphur flung his six gun. It caught the renegade alongside the head. With a groan he stiffened and then slumped down, out when he struck the floor.

"Much obliged, Sulphur," Jim gritted. Even as he spoke he was searching the room with his eyes. He saw Carlotta, bound in her chair. A single long step took him to her side.

"Are you hurt?" he exclaimed as he whipped out a knife and slashed her bonds.

"No, Jim," she answered with surprising calm. "But I think you came just in time—"

She broke off abruptly as her eyes fell on Quan Goon, who had just stepped in the door. The hard-faced Chinese fastened an accusative eye on her. Jim thought he saw the girl pale slightly.

With that one glimpse of Quan Goon Carlotta seemed to understand that circumstances were different from what she had supposed.

"Moy Quai, we have come for you," the powerful Quan announced. He made it sound like a threat.

"Yes," she murmured submissively. "I am ready to go."

They were just emerging from the building when a hoarse shout was raised from the direction of the gate. It was Happy Failes.

"My God, hustle!" he screeched. "Here comes Salters an' his whole damn gang! They'll wipe us out if they ketch us here! There must be a dozen of 'em!"

Jim sprang that way, less to confirm Happy's words than to estimate how much time they had in which to effect their escape. But it was already too late. Only a few hundred yards away a grimly determined cavalcade was galloping up, rifles at the ready. At their head rode Slade Salters.

10

Sulphur Riley had his look at the oncoming men. His face was longer than ever when he turned. "Jim, we're in a jack pot!" he cried, his voice hoarse with apprehension.

"Close the gate," Jim jerked out. "Quick, before they notice anything!"

Sulphur complied without comment. But he

gave Morningstar a questioning look as together they jammed the heavy bars in place.

"They'll expect the gate to be closed," Jim explained swiftly, "and it'll hold them up a few minutes longer. Even if they heard the shooting here in the fort, they can't be sure of what's going on."

"What difference does that make?" Sulphur countered. "There ain't but one way out o' here—an' that's straight through them birds!"

"You're wrong," was the prompt retort. "I didn't go all the way through this place without noticing a small gate in the rear stockade. It's double-barred and locked, and it opens on the creek bed. We'll leave that way and make a break as soon as we get in the open. It doesn't seem possible that we can slip away without being spotted, but we'll have to take the chance!"

A few words sufficed to acquaint the Chinese with what was to be attempted. Even as they started for the rear gate Slade Salters' men reached the main entrance. There was a banging on the outside with the butt of a gun, and then a voice bellowed:

"Hey, Tupper! Open up here!"

Jim motioned his party to hurry. Sulphur and Johnnie were already at the rear gate, working frantically to get it open. The lock delayed them. Quan Goon and his fierce desert riders stared back in the direction of the main gate, expressions of anger twisting their visages. Jim guessed how ready they were to face Salters' force regardless of numbers or consequences. His eye caught Carlotta's appealing glance.

"Tell your friends we haven't a chance if we make the slightest mistake now," he said quickly. "I'd like to square things with Salters myself—but this simply isn't the time!"

Carlotta nodded almost coldly. He would have wondered about that, except for watching the effect of her words as she spoke to the Chinese in swift, rippling syllables. They scowled, but it was plain the girl's argument was having some effect. At length Quan Goon turned to Jim. "All right," he muttered. "You lead the way—and make no mistakes!"

Sulphur got the gate open just as a louder uproar from across the compound warned that Salters and the others would not wait much longer, that already their suspicions were aroused.

"Git this gate open, Tupper, before we kick it down!" came the bull roar of a heavy, authoritative voice.

Jim said quietly: "Now, get through and go into the creek bed! We'll have to move quick if we don't want to be closed off altogether. Quick, and quietly!"

The gate had been cut low. It was necessary to lead the horses through before mounting. Sulphur was the last man outside. He turned to Morningstar.

"What about Cache Tupper?" he demanded. "He'll have the main gate open an' them buzzards told the truth in no time."

"No matter," was the crisp response. "We couldn't hope for a delay of more than a few minutes. . . . Fork your bronc and lead off!"

The course of their flight was clearly indicated to them. Only by following the winding bed of Furnace Creek could they hope for any cover whatever.

Sulphur led the way. Quan Goon's men followed, with Carlotta well shielded. Morningstar and the other punchers brought up the rear. Jim could hardly fail to notice that the dark slanting glances of the Chinese were everywhere; nor was there ever a moment when they were not in full command of the situation.

What could it mean? he asked himself. He had helped them to free Carlotta, proof enough that he had had nothing to do with her abduction. And yet, would the matter end here? Bill Merriam rode up beside him before he found the answer.

"Just where does this leave us, Morningstar, and what about Miss Orme?" He jerked his chin toward the Chinese. "They'll never let Carlotta take us to her."

"Afraid you're right," Jim admitted frankly. "Our only hope is to get the jump on them if a chance offers."

Almost before he had ceased speaking a noisy

uproar from the direction of the fort whirled them around. And now Jim had reason to be thankful that the moon, almost at the full tonight, had already dropped low in the western sky. Around the corner of the post stockade came streaming a sharply silhouetted string of horsemen which seemed never to end. They circled sharply, until a harsh cry was raised from the creek bed. Sure of the scent then, they swept toward the quarry at a gallop.

"Here they come!" Jim heard Happy Failes's rifled exclamation. "My God! Bronc Yeager's gang is ridin' with 'em!"

Morningstar knew what that spelled, but for the moment all his attention was fastened on seeing that his party made the best possible speed. Even so, it was only a matter of moments before a slug whistled past his head and another stung Johnnie's bronc on the flank. Landers whirled angrily, unlimbering his gun. It blazed toward the renegades without materially slackening their pursuit.

In another moment the Chinese got into the fight. That they could shoot as well as ride Jim soon learned; rifles freckled the night with flame, and at least one owlhoot was dumped unceremoniously when his bronc dropped out from under him.

Jim worked his way toward Carlotta. A glance told him the girl was all right. She, too, could ride when it became a necessity, and she was riding now. "Try and keep between her and those lobos behind us," he called to the punchers. "Don't let a slug find her."

The pursuit was pressing close now. The renegades clearly outnumbered Carlotta's rescuers and were counting on that fact. Their bullets screamed closer and closer, until Bill Merriam, for one, was beginning to wonder where this affair would end.

He had not long to wait for his answer. For some moments he had noted that Morningstar seemed working toward some definite objective. Now Bill saw what it was. Ahead a sharp ridge rose, edging the sky blackly, and through it Furnace Creek cut like a knife. Straight toward the gap the fugitives pressed their ponies. Merriam stared for a moment at the lofty granite walls of the gorge; then he jerked a question:

"One man could hold that gap forever. But can we hope to make it, Morningstar?"

Jim didn't bother to answer. Only time could do that, and its answer would be conclusive.

"They're wise to what we're up to," Sulphur jerked out. "They'll cut us off if they can."

"Don't let them," Jim jerked out sharply. He fired as he spoke, aiming at a man on the far right as the renegades sought to spread out and enclose them in a net. There wasn't much farther to go now. Another three minutes and they rode

115

into the shadow of the rocky walls. A last fierce fusillade, and pursuit was left behind.

Jim nodded approval as Quan Goon spoke to two of his warriors and gestured backward. The Chinese drew in, turning their ponies. It was dark here in the gorge; Jim felt the pair would be reasonably secure even though no cover afforded save the broken walls. It was only a moment before the men dropped from sight as he and the others rode on at a steady, space-covering gait.

Less than five minutes had passed, however, before a crash of shots broke out sharply, echoing weirdly from the rocks. Jim tossed a glance at Quan Goon. The Oriental caught it.

"Don't worry," he assured with impregnable calm. "They will not get through."

That wasn't what was worrying Jim. "They'll swing around that ridge," he responded. "A matter of two hours or better. But their broncs are fresh."

Quan Goon nodded. "That 'll be time enough."

They had not gone more than a mile or two through the rough, broken country beyond the ridge when, at a guttural word from Quan Goon, the party swerved away from the creek bed. Jim was about to protest this striking off into deep sand, which would quickly wear down the ponies, when it occurred to him that daylight was not many hours off. This sandy plain was perhaps the one sure means at hand of effectually covering all trace of their passing. The dawn breeze would quickly obliterate their tracks.

It was a hope of safety not without its price, for only a matter of minutes had passed before the ponies began to labor. The sand might stretch for miles. Morningstar set the example by dismounting and starting to lead his bronc. Sulphur, Merriam, Johnnie and Hap followed suit, and, after a delay, Carlotta did likewise despite the protests of both Jim and Quan Goon. But the Chinese showed no evidence of any intention to favor their horses.

"Cold-blooded devils," Sulphur muttered to Jim in an undertone. The latter shrugged.

"It's their way," he said. "No use to argue with them."

Quan Goon drifted toward them at the moment as if by accident. His suspicions of treachery were leaping. Jim said no more.

In moon-silvered desolation the party pressed southward toward distant serrated ridges which seemed never to draw nearer. At last the sand ended. Jim swung into the saddle with relief. As he was about to go on Quan Goon and another Chinese closed in on him with calm and machinelike precision. No word was spoken, but Jim found himself relieved of his guns with an adeptness that would have done credit to many a lawman. The same thing was happening to Sulphur, Merriam and the rest of the whites. It was Jim's first intimation that their captors considered them safe from pursuit.

"Hold on," Jim protested. He faced Quan Goon. "You've got Miss Soong safe; that was our agreement. It's up to some of us to go back now and give the sheriff a hand. We wouldn't have got very far tonight except for him."

Quan Goon heard him out, flinty of face. He started to shake a cold negative, when Carlotta unexpectedly put in a word.

"The sheriff unwittingly did us a favor, but he will have to get out of his difficulties the best way he can," she said decisively. He stared at her in surprise.

"What do you mean?" he countered. "All that has been done was in your interests. . . ."

"And against my express wishes. Later in the day you will be at liberty to leave, and my advice would be to return to town."

Jim was dumfounded. Yet he understood well enough that Carlotta was incensed because she believed he had betrayed her confidence. He exclaimed: "Are you forgetting your promise to take me to Miss Orme?"

"We both made promises in Piute," she reminded him. "Yours is already broken."

Morningstar noticed that the Chinese were beginning to get excited. They stared at him and then talked together in rapid-fire fashion. Carlotta listened for a moment and seemed to come to some decision. She turned to Quan Goon.

Jim didn't know what they were saying to each other, but, judging from the flow of talk and the gestures, it was to the point. The girl could only be trying to persuade Quan Goon to let them go. It was not going so well with her either; Jim sensed dimly that there were forces at play here bigger than her.

It did not escape him that she might even be endangering her own life in doing what she was attempting. It was incomprehensible, coming on top of her distrust of him of a few minutes before, and yet it did not conflict with the enigma of her strange personality.

Sulphur edged near to Jim while the latter waited. Lowering his voice, he muttered: "Damned if I like the looks uh this, Jim. We don't stand a ghost of a show, the way things stack up, but we never let that stop us before. . . . Why not try to grab a gun an' make a break? We can take our chances of some of us gittin' through!"

Jim reflected briefly. He was dubious of their ability to get the upper hand of these yellow riders. He shook his head slowly.

"If it was only ourselves it wouldn't matter so much, but Merriam and Carlotta would be over their heads," he answered guardedly. "And there's Miss Orme to consider too. We'll string along for now."

Sulphur grunted disparagingly but made no

protest. The heated discussion between Quan Goon and the girl ended at that moment, and the latter turned to Jim.

"I have been trying to get permission for you all to leave and join the sheriff," she said. "I didn't succeed. But one of you may go. That will be you, Jim. You will be given your rifle and some canteens. When you find those men take them out of the desert at once. Do not return here. Do you understand?"

Jim was not sure that he did, but for Quan Goon's benefit he nodded as if in full approval. It was the signal for an immediate change of attitude toward him. One of the Chinese handed over his rifle. Several canteens of water were hung on his saddle horn.

"Don't try any tricks," was Quan Goon's parting speech, his look fierce and unrelenting. "You'll pay for it with your life if you do. Go!"

Jim needed no urging to accept the hint. But first he turned to Sulphur and the others. "I'll find Mulhall," he told them. "Things may work out all right."

They might read what they chose into that. He took his pony's bridle and started to turn away. He was about to swing into the saddle when a voice stopped him.

"Jim!"

It was Carlotta. She had followed him. Reaching his side, she did not pause but went on in calm silence. Together they drew away from the others, to stop only when they were alone, ringed in by the desolate wastes; the declining moon, huge and red as it neared the horizon, gazed at them as if with a wisdom older than theirs.

"What is it, Carlotta?" he asked, his tone grave.

"I—I couldn't let you go like this . . . without a word," she murmured. Their glances held. "Jim—I overheard part of what you said to your man Sulphur. I know you are brave. Please don't be foolish. Don't try to come back. I can't guarantee your safety if you do."

Looking at her, Morningstar found her lips touched with sadness. The moonlight seemed to enhance her rare beauty.

"The boys—Doctor Merriam—what is to become of them?" he demanded. She hesitated over her answer and her magnificent poise seemed to break.

"I don't know. For the present they will have to go with us. I shall try to convince Quan that it would be the better part of wisdom to set them free. He's afraid they know too much."

He caught her hand and made her look at him.

"Carlotta, you'll never convince him, nor will he ever permit you to free Jennifer Orme. There's a pair of yellow devils in his eyes. He hates all whites. I've often heard of the Chinese bandit crew that terrorized central Nevada in the years that followed that miserable business at Union

City. Quan Goon is a throwback to that bunch."

"Hardly a throwback," she said. "He is one of them. . . . He rode with those men. The abuses and injustice he and his countrymen endured in those old gold camp days still burn like a white flame in his mind. There are times when some of us would forget. Always we have Quan to remind us."

Her tone was bitter again, and it carried a vague hostility even for him. She withdrew her hand. Regarding her closely, Morningstar realized that for the moment she was all Chinese.

"Carlotta, you told me in Piute that yours was not the only voice in the Wu-tai-shan Company. Those other voices are speaking now, aren't they? I believe you were sincere in your intention to return Miss Orme to Piute through me. For that reason you are now in danger yourself."

"It is nothing," she insisted.

"No, Carlotta, you can't deceive me," he said. "You are just as much a prisoner as Sulphur and the others." Thought of the fate that had befallen Doy Kee came to him and tightened his mouth. "You are helpless, maybe actually in danger."

She smiled at his earnestness. "Quan does only what he thinks is best," she murmured. "He, too, is responsible to the Wu-tai-shan Company." Morningstar found something in her tone that was far from a note of resignation before the inevitable.

"Jim—you are risking your life in trying to find

the sheriff and his men," she warned. "I think you understand Slade Salters' purpose as well as I do. Greed has turned him into a madman. There's no turning back for him now. He's risked everything on this toss of the dice. There's nothing he'll stop at."

"It isn't likely a man will stop at anything when he takes to running with renegades and outlaws. Obviously, he is playing for a big stake."

"Obviously," Carlotta echoed without hesitation. Her dark eyes had a dangerous gleam. "He will pay for his treachery and stupidity. We shall know how—" She broke off abruptly. Morningstar felt her eyes questioning him. "Jim—I am a woman. I know that the hope that I would lead you to Jennifer Orme was not the least of the reasons why you stopped at nothing to find me. I think I understand your interest in her—perhaps better than you do yourself."

He would have interrupted, but she was not through.

"Jim, there's nothing you can do. You'll have to depend on me. If you really want to help her see to it that the sheriff does nothing further."

Morningstar could only shake his head. "You are asking the impossible," he said. "Mulhall is no fool. You'll never keep the law out of the affairs of the Wu-tai-shan Company now."

"We shall find a way!" A voice swung him around. Quan Goon stood there, fierce, implacable. "Dead men make trouble for no one!"

11

Starting back through the sand the way he had come, Morningstar's first thought was of Slade Salters and his men. Thrown off the trail they might be, but that did not mean they were defeated. Somewhere ahead he could expect to run into them. Dealing with them single-handed would be a different matter from facing them in company with upward of a dozen seasoned fighting men.

Before he had gone a mile he had the dragging, unstable sand to fight. He fought it in the only way that held any chance of success: slowly, steadily, with endless patience. Before long he was once more on foot, leading the way, while his bronc plodded after, head swinging. The moon had dipped below the horizon, leaving black velvet darkness, starshot, cold. There was nothing for it but to keep going, but the events of the past twelve hours had left him with plenty to think about.

The fact that Slade Salters had so recklessly burned his bridges behind him was less of a surprise to Jim than that the attorney had found reason to seek the support of a large force of fighting men. Jim knew Bronc Yeager well enough to understand that there must indeed be a big stake at issue to have interested the owlhoot. All things considered, it was easy enough to believe in the existence of the mysterious gold mine of which Clay Masters had hinted. One thing was certain: there was either a fabulously rich mine somewhere in the rimrock flanking the Fortifications or else some even richer prize.

The fact made it possible to understand at last what had happened to Jennifer Orme. She had not been the victim of some fantastic plot aimed at herself; rather, she had had the misfortune to become involved in this greater game.

He knew dawn could not be far off. Soon the sky began to brighten in the east. But, as with everything else about this night, not even its end was like the ending of other nights. Instead of bringing the bright promise of a new day, the sun rose red and sullen. And now he became aware of the breathless, almost suffocating stillness of the air, the dread waiting of a sinister something lying just below the sky line. He knew better than to attribute it to the appalling silence of this desert; it was more than that. Watching with apprehension the gradual thickening of the sky to the north, he realized that it was flying sand.

"She'll tear things loose when she hits!" he burst out. His patience snapped. "Damn such hellish luck! I'm not going to get anywhere in this!"

Had cover of any kind afforded, he would

have gotten the bronc and himself under protection till the storm blew itself out, whatever the delay. But there was not even a broken ledge in sight. The line of desolate hills which a few moments before had marched across the horizon to the north had already been blotted out.

There came to his ears a low and gloomy moaning. It was the wind. The moan rose in pitch to a wail; a scouring, gritty breeze brushed Jim's cheek. The air near at hand began to thicken. As if by force of suggestion, his lips suddenly felt dry, but, wiping them, he found a few particles of sand clinging to them already.

Hastily he took his bearings before everything was blotted out by the descending pall. Fortunately he was able at a distance of a quarter mile to identify the straggling, dry bed of Furnace Creek. He thought: "I'll stick to it. It will take me to where I heard Mulhall's guns popping."

The storm closed down a moment later, lashing him with its gritty tongue. Dismounting and stumbling on, leading the bronc, he was afraid he had either overshot or swung away from the dry wash. He was on the point of halting where he was, when his boots slid down a slight pitch and he realized he had reached Furnace Creek.

The flying sand had darkened the sky to a murky dusk. Half by luck, and half by some sixth sense, he stuck to the shallow creek bed. Moving at a snail's pace, several hours passed before a looming shadow ahead presaged the break in the ridge not far from Mormon Fort. But if he had hoped for protection there he was disappointed. The storm swirled through the gorge with increased vigor, if anything. Head lowered against the blast, he fought his way through, his eyes red-rimmed above the raised neckerchief that protected his face.

He knew he was not far from where Huck Mulhall and his deputies had made their stand. From the first Morningstar had asked himself exactly what the sheriff's movements could have been after being attacked by Slade's crowd. The agreement had been that he and Mulhall should meet at the headwaters of Furnace Creek—a matter of some miles to the north of this point. Though it was improbable that Mulhall knew anything of what had happened at the fort, it was only reasonable to suppose he surmised that the men who had attacked him had come from there. Outnumbered, some of his men undoubtedly wounded, if not killed, it was unlikely that he would drive on toward the upper reaches of the creek, though he still stood desperately in need of the water he could hope only to procure there.

"He's undoubtedly dropping back toward Piute this minute," Morningstar decided. "If I'm to find him it will be off to the west somewhere."

He took it for granted that Salters' renegades had returned to the fort before the storm struck.

When another hour passed, with no sign of the storm slacking off, he felt that the time had come for him to pull up until he could get his bearings.

His pony turned tail to the blast when he stopped. It was like creating a little eddy in the bedlam of the elements. Even as he paused Morningstar thought he caught the faint, wind-shredded sound of gunshots and then hoarse shouting. He was about to dismiss it, believing it no more than the work of his imagination, when it came again.

"It's Mulhall!" he exclaimed. "He and his men have become separated or something."

Pausing only long enough to make certain of the direction, he started off. For a time faith drew him on. There was only the dismal moan of the storm to reward him. At last he halted in perplexity. "Guess they weren't over this way after all."

Again he bent every faculty to catch that elusive sound of human making. As if the storm found delight in being contrary, the wailing of the wind rose in a screeching crescendo; he could have heard no other sound had it been there. Waiting for a lull, he started to work across the wind. Suddenly he drew his horse in with a jerk.

There it was again—the muffled, faint crack of a gun, followed by a hoarse call! This time he refused to listen to the suggestions of fancy, pressing squarely into the teeth of the wind. He had his reward in the infrequent repetition of those signals, still distant and baffling, but stronger than before.

Suddenly he plainly caught the sound of two men crying out to each other. It was impossible to recognize the voices, but he felt certain that, by a miraculous chance, he had found Mulhall and his deputies. Raising his rifle, he fired it skyward three times and then, after a pause, thrice more.

An answering shout reached him. And then the storm veil tore apart to show him a man not twenty yards away. What he saw was so unexpected that he could only sit tight and stare, while the truth hammered at his brain with the weight of blows from a sledge. This was not Huck Mulhall; it was Slade Salters!

Salters was no less startled. As Morningstar whirled his bronc to start away Slade whipped up his gun and fired at almost point-blank range. The bullet droned close.

"Here's one of 'em, boys!" Salters yelled. "It's Morningstar! Don't let him get away!"

There was an answering shout, a rush of hoofs. Jim did not hesitate for long, jamming his horse ahead sharply and trusting to luck.

After that one swirling rent which afforded him a glimpse of Salters the storm had dropped its impenetrable curtain again. Morningstar was beginning to believe he was making good his escape when, without warning, a horseman materialized before him, blocking his path. There wasn't time to swerve aside. Jim didn't try. At the moment of collision he rose in the stirrups and swung at the other man.

The rider managed to get out a short sharp yelp of surprise before the blow caught him alongside the jaw and tumbled him out of the saddle as if roped. His frightened bronc started away and in three strides disappeared in the storm.

Morningstar changed course again slightly and drove on. The sand slashed at him, the wind roared in his ears. But twenty minutes later he drew up, safe in the knowledge that he had given Salters and his men the slip.

His whereabouts a mystery now, he knew there was nothing for it but to hole up somewhere and wait for the storm to blow itself out. Accordingly, he let himself drift with the wind, as the simplest course, trying to keep track of how much ground he was covering. He came at length to a high rocky ridge too steep and rugged to climb. But along its base lay a reef of rocks. In the lee of it he stopped. Climbing stiffly out of the saddle, he raised a canteen to his lips and washed out his mouth. He settled himself to wait then. This storm might blow for another hour, or it might continue for several days. There was no telling how soon his release would come.

Thinking of Mulhall, he was surprised to find that he knew exactly what he wanted to tell him.

His own course seemed just as surprisingly clear. He recalled what Carlotta had said concerning his interest in Jennifer. It was something he was reluctant to face. He even tried to deny that she meant anything to him. He told himself their ways lay a million miles apart.

"I won't permit myself to indulge in any foolish dreaming of that sort," he muttered. "Merriam is the man for her; they have a lot in common—their work—their background, too, I guess."

He wondered what had been in Carlotta's mind when she spoke. From the first, her attitude toward Miss Orme had been one of mingled contempt and pity. He accepted it as the natural bitterness of a girl of mixed blood toward all white women. It completely escaped him that, in this instance, he figured importantly; that Carlotta recognized a dangerous rival for his affections in Jennifer Orme. Had he suspected the truth, he would have found fresh cause for anxiety.

A slight slackening in the fury of the gale aroused him from his abstraction. Twenty minutes later he was convinced that the storm was passing. As the wind fell the sand began to sift earthward from the murky pall above him. Gradually the sky lightened. He could see about him again. His field of vision widened swiftly.

After a little reconnoitering he was able to climb up on the ridge. From its crest he could command a wide view of the barren waste.

It lacked an hour of noon when he spotted a number of men ahead on weary ponies. It was not long before he had satisfied himself that they were Mulhall and his deputies. A shot fired in the air served to turn them and then bring them in his direction as he advanced.

"Wal, Morningstar—I was wonderin' what happened to yuh," was the sheriff's gruff greeting. "We had a gun fight that was a honey while she lasted." His eye sharpened as he noted the canteens swinging from Jim's saddle horn. "Where's Merriam an' the others?"

"They're somewhere between here and Pueblo Grande," was Jim's sober response. "They're in a jack pot for sure this time!" He handed over the canteens. Mulhall and hi parched and jaded men slaked their thirst.

"Suppose it was the bunch that jumped us that picked 'em up," the sheriff growled. Anger boiled in him at thought of what he and his men had walked into. "Salters has got Bronc Yeager's bunch ridin' with him now. That's why he got off the stage an' headed north."

"I know," Morningstar nodded. "We had a running fight with them. But it's not them this time. A big war party of fighting Chinks is hustling my boys south across this desert."

"Chinks?" Mulhall exclaimed. "A big bunch of 'em, eh? By jabors, this desert seems to be crawlin' with men!" He beckoned Morningstar aside. "Now you talk fast an' tell me jest what happened since I saw yuh last. I want to get to the bottom of this."

Convinced that he must confide in Mulhall—as much for Carlotta's sake as his own, irrespective of what she had said—Jim gave him a detailed account of the happenings of the night, from the moment that Quan Goon and his yellow riders had surprised them, through the attack on Mormon Fort, the releasing of Carlotta, the running fight down Furnace Creek and the circumstances that led to his turning back in search of the sheriff.

Mulhall was choking with surprise at the end. A few moments later questions were popping off his tongue. "You say this girl Carlotta is in danger from her own crowd now?"

Jim nodded. "She doesn't think so, but I do. I saw what happened to one member of the Wu-tai-shan Company who fell into disfavor." He told Mulhall about Doy Kee. "That may well be the fate that's awaiting her."

"I'm damned if it don't pass belief!" Huck exploded. "Dead men—kidnapin'—armed renegades naggin' away at yuh! And yet they say nothin' happens in this county! Don't need a sheriff, they think!" He ripped out an oath that gave eloquent proof of the state of his feelings. "What's your answer to this, Morningstar?" he demanded. "You must have some idea of what it all means."

"A rich mine—Indian treasure," Jim answered. "It's as near as I can come. It's only a guess."

Huck shook his head. "I don't know," he muttered. "Men can't git along without water and grub, whether they're yellow or white. Ain't no water in the Fortification Mountains. Ain't no game—not even a jackrabbit. Makes me think it must be sunthin' else."

"Whatever it is—I aim to find out," Jim said soberly. "The best way to do it is to overtake that crowd before they reach Pueblo Grande and disappear, maybe forever. Why do you think they're holding Miss Orme, Mulhall? Certainly not because she can be of any use to them. She knows too much. That's all. They know if they release her their secret goes with her. It 'll be the same with Merriam and my boys—to say nothing of Carlotta. If we're going to do anything for them we've got to do it in a hurry."

"But take a look at my men, Morningstar!" Mulhall protested. "Jensen's got a slug in his shoulder. Bill Vetters' got a smashed wrist. You can't go draggin' men around the desert in their condition. . . . No," he continued in an even more decided tone, "my move is to head back to town at once. We'll git fresh horses and organize a big posse. We can do this thing right then."

"But that 'll be a matter of days, Mulhall!" Jim protested. "If it's got to be one man against a dozen, okay! I'll be that man. I'm heading for Pueblo Grande."

"Morningstar, don't be a fool!" Huck snorted. "I won't let the grass grow under my feet, but it will be three, four days before I can git there. You'll need grub and water. I can give you a little grain for your hoss, but that's all."

"I'll make out," Jim told him. "I buried a keg of water against such an emergency as this when the expedition broke camp. As for the grub—I'll get along with what I've got."

A few minutes later, with Mulhall repeating his promise to reach the ruins at the earliest possible moment, Morningstar rode away. He wasn't interested in trying to read sign or pick up the trail of Quan Goon's party. His goal was the old pueblo, and with uncanny accuracy he held true to his course all that long day.

The sun was low when the rimrock above Pueblo Grande hove into view. Nearing the old base camp, he purposely swung off to the west. In an arroyo he hobbled his pony and went on afoot. Believing he was well ahead of Quan Goon's party, he planned to take up a position on a rocky ledge that commanded a view of the mesquite-dotted draw, down which anyone coming from the north must travel.

As he was in the act of dropping to his knees, preparatory to stretching out on the ledge, something struck him in the back and knocked him flat. Savage yellow hands grabbed him. His rifle was kicked beyond reach. A tangle of grunting Chinese swarmed over him as he fought furiously. From nowhere a boot lashed out in a murderous kick which narrowly missed his head.

Morningstar knew no word of Chinese, but a cry was raised and repeated again and again; translated into good English, he knew it could be nothing less than "Kill the spy!"

The wicked glint of a knife at his throat convinced him that it was useless to struggle further. In no time his wrists were lashed together and he was roughly dragged to his feet and ordered to march down the draw.

A matter of several hundred yards brought him and his captors into sight of the old base camp. There stood Bill Merriam and the boys. Their hands were being bound with as little ceremony as he had received. Plainly, his reappearance had enraged Quan Goon and brought this indignity down on his white prisoners.

While Morningstar stood there, soberly contemplating his wrecked plans, Carlotta appeared. The reproach in her eyes was tempered by her concern for him.

"Why did you come back?" she exclaimed. "I warned you not to try it."

He met her troubled gaze with a serenity he was far from feeling. "I had to play it this way," he told her simply. With Quan Goon's men

136

ringing him in, watching him like hawks, their yellow faces inscrutable and forbidding, he offered no further explanation.

Carlotta gazed at him with something akin to awe in her dark eyes. "You brave, foolish man!" she said. "Does your life mean so little to you?" The question, so pregnant with sinister meaning, seemed wrenched from her lips. "Jim, this was madness!"

12

A husky, flat-faced Chinese stepped up beside Morningstar and laid a rough hand on him. "Come," he grunted. He thrust Jim in the direction of the pueblo. The other followed.

At this sunset hour the great ruin lay bathed in liquid amber light, almost unearthly in its somber grandeur, the citadel of a long-departed glory, but symbolizing still the mystery and the sadness of life. There was an even deeper meaning in the scene for Morningstar, for somewhere in the vast broken area of cracked and weathered cliffs, crags and deep-shadowed canyons rising behind the ruin Jennifer was being held prisoner, waiting, longing—perhaps daily expecting the belated arrival of help.

Jim was dragged back from his thoughts by the

sound of Sulphur's voice. The lanky one had edged toward him. "What in hell are yuh doin' back here, Jim?" he muttered. His tone revealed the gravity with which he viewed the situation.

"Mulhall couldn't come with me. I couldn't leave you like this," Jim answered hurriedly. The Chinese thrust them apart before they could say more.

Mounting to the pueblo, the prisoners were led toward a large adobe room on its edge. In its ancient entrance Morningstar saw a figure appear. It was Quan Goon. The Oriental's harsh face twisted up with sudden fury at sight of him.

"You have come back—hoping to spy on us!" he threw at Jim flatly. His wrath rose in a red tide of hate. "Foolish dog of a white! You choose to throw your life away—or perhaps you think you will be spared!" Fathomless contempt rang in his tone; his glare was one of unleashed ferocity.

Morningstar was taken aback by the savageness of it. For once he found himself wordless. He had never seen a more sinister figure. Quan Goon personified the ageless Tartar hatred of the yellow blood for the white; once his racial instincts took charge there would be no slightest impulse of humanity in him. The fate his crafty brain was even now preparing for Jim might well include Sulphur, Merriam and the others. It was a sobering thought.

Before Morningstar could collect his wits

Carlotta attempted to interpose hurriedly. Quan whirled on her. "Silence!" he thundered, his scowl attesting to his change of attitude toward her, if that were needed. "There will be no more talk. You persuaded me before against my better judgment, Moy Quai. It will not happen again!"

"For God's sake, Morningstar, can't you do something to appease him?" Merriam demanded hoarsely. "He'll slit the throats of all of us if he isn't brought to his senses!"

"Pull yourself together," Jim advised, when he caught Quan Goon's fierce eyes fastened on him. They seemed to dart lightning. The flat yellow lips parted and lashing words came.

"You were warned what the penalty would be if you disobeyed!" He was about to pass sentence now. Unconsciously Jim stiffened.

"You can kill me, Quan," he made answer thinly. "I can't do anything to prevent it. But it will be your last mistake; I'll promise you that!"

The Oriental appeared to grow in stature; the thick cords of his bronzed neck swelled with rage. His fingers worked convulsively on the haft of the knife at his waist. In this tense moment anything could happen; Jim had about given himself up for a dead man when a swift gust of murmuring ran through Quan Goon's yellow followers which attracted the latter's attention. Wheeling sharply, he barked a harsh query in Chinese.

The answer came swiftly. Morningstar's gaze flashed to the man who gave it, posted at the end of a gallery a score of yards away. Gesturing beyond, as though pointing at something, he let loose a stream of words. His obvious excitement was quickly communicated to the others. Morningstar understood in a flash that someone was coming.

A glance at Quan Goon confirmed it. Moreover, Quan's momentary expression of uncertainty said that whoever it might be it was a personage of importance. A moment later several expressionless Chinese, armed to the teeth, put in an appearance. Quan's men greeted them gravely; but, scrutinizing each one keenly, Morningstar realized they were but the bodyguards of whoever was coming.

When the man appeared, dignified of bearing, shrewd eyed, with an impassive yellow mask of a face, Jim knew he was right. It was Sui Chen, the bland importer who had brought so much weight to bear in the Wu-tai-shan Company's conferences in Reno; but, beyond a vague feeling of familiarity, which he failed to identify, Morningstar did not place him. There could be little question of his authority here, however. Quan Goon awaited his approach, obviously chafing at the interruption.

When Quan would have burst out in a torrent of hot words Sui Chen cut him off with quiet decision. "Words spoken in haste are devoid of wisdom," he said in their own tongue, yet with the rebuke in his tone plain for all to read. "Hasty actions are no more to be commended."

Quan's visage was thunderous with baffled fury, but he did not retort. Sui Chen turned calmly to Jim.

"You are Jim Morningstar," he said, with no trace of accent in his words. "I am sorry to find you in this position; there has been a series of mistakes here." And to one of his men, indicating Jim, Sulphur and the others, he said: "Release these people at once!"

The tranquil dignity of this elderly Oriental as he took the situation in hand was genuine; Jim realized it afresh, watching his glance flick to Carlotta for the first time. Sui Chen might have fully expected to find her here for all the reaction he showed. Certainly he was not surprised, although he must have known of her abduction. The smile he gave her was gentle, kindly. Before he could speak Quan Goon, unable to contain himself longer, fired off a wrathy blast that came like a thunderclap.

"It is you who make the mistake, Sui Chen, in striking the bonds from these dogs of whites!" he charged, hostility boiling into his arrogant visage. "Freedom is not what they deserve at our hands!" He drove on with fierce energy, shooting a look of hatred and distrust at

Morningstar as he stated his grievance; describing how Jim had demanded his release on the pretext of aiding Sheriff Mulhall; how he had been given canteens of water and warned not to come back on pain of death. Anger running away with him, he whirled on Jim.

"But you came back!" he thundered. "You were spying on us—trying to learn our secrets! Why did you come? Who sent you? Was it Mulhall?" He threw the words like bullets. Jim sensed the gathering excitement of his listeners, read his design of carrying them with him. Suddenly the harsh voice rose. "Vermin, jackal, son of turtles—you are working with that man!"

"I'm working neither for nor against Mulhall," Jim tossed back flatly. "You can get that out of your head. It's the law that matters here! You've managed to keep it out of your calculations for years, but that's over and done with now. Secrecy is one thing, but plotting—abduction—murder!" He shook his head. "Even in this desert you can't cover up things like that."

Quan Goon would have retorted hotly, but Sui Chen silenced him with a word. Addressing the latter, Jim went on:

"I realize that you have every reason to hate me; in your eyes my very name is against me. But I'm not interested in your secret. In trying to protect yourselves you're standing in your own way! It's known that you people are here in

142

the desert now. These mysterious disappearances won't be passed over; sooner or later they'll spell your finish."

Sui Chen nodded gravely. His broad face might have been carved from ivory, devoid of expression as it was. "You speak wisely, my friend," he said.

"Mr Morningstar scarcely does himself justice," Carlotta broke in quietly. "Quan Goon has neglected to tell you what he did for me." She described Jim's share in the fight at Mormon Fort. Sui Chen listened attentively to the end. As near as his expression could be read, it was one of approval. He turned to Jim once more.

"You have more to say, I think," he suggested.

Morningstar had. He was only waiting to get it off his chest. "Turning back on your present course, undoing what harm you can, is your only chance," he declared. "You'll have to return Miss Orme and let us all leave. . . . The killing of Doy Kee is another matter—but you can go a long way toward squaring even that."

Sui Chen glanced at Quan and then at Carlotta, asking a silent question; whatever the answers were, he was satisfied. "We will consider these things," he said.

At a sign from him they started to move apart. Morningstar knew they meant to confer together. Quan Goon, still hot-tempered and suspicious, burst into vehement argument. Sui Chen and Carlotta reasoned with him firmly. It was not easy to tell which way the discussion was going.

Bill Merriam grew restless as the minutes dragged out. "I appreciate your concern for Miss Orme, Morningstar!" he burst out finally, his hostility apparent. "If it wasn't so absurd I'd say your interest in her was personal. . . . Or is it so absurd?"

Jim whirled on him. His nerves were strung tighter than he knew. But the same thing was true of them all. He checked the hot retort trembling on his tongue. "You don't know what you're saying, Merriam. You'd better consider your words more carefully," he advised.

"I've had plenty of time to think them over!" Merriam threw back angrily. "It hasn't escaped me that you've been worrying more about her than about the rest of us!"

Jim stared at him for a moment. "What do you mean?" he rasped in an edged tone. "Do you think I shouldn't?" But listening as Merriam drifted off into evasive recriminations, he thought he knew what was bothering the man. It wasn't Jennifer's well-being at the moment, or even his interest in her, so much as the fact that Bill resented being relegated to the background in this discussion with the Chinese. A moment later the proof came of his injured feelings.

"I don't know why I didn't take matters in my own hands from the beginning," he jerked out bitterly. "If I had we might have got some results by this time; but instead, here we are, still helpless: depending on the favor of this bunch of yellow cutthroats—"

"Keep your tongue between your teeth!" Morningstar cut him off curtly. "How far do you think we'll get if one of these Chinese overhears that kind of talk?"

Merriam's answer was a wrathy glare. For a moment it looked as if he meant to swing on Jim. Then he wilted, groaning: "You got me into this—I suppose I'll have to string along. But, God, how I hate it!" He flung away.

Sulphur exchanged glances with Morningstar and shrugged. "The sand in that gent's craw is wearin' thin," he grunted.

At the moment Jim saw Sui Chen and the others turn his way. The stout Oriental was inscrutable as ever; Quan Goon still scowled blackly. But Carlotta's beautiful face, in which Jim hoped to read his answer at once, was utterly expressionless.

"My friend, we have agreed that the course you suggest is the one to follow." It was Sui Chen who spoke. "It will not be easy. But it is the only thing that will redeem us with your white law."

Jim's stern mouth softened in a smile of satisfaction at the words. "You are wise," he nodded.

Bill Merriam broke in then. "Just where does this leave us?" he demanded bluntly.

"You will be given your guns," Sui Chen

assured him. He transferred his attention to Morningstar. "You and your friends will remain here. Miss Orme will be brought to you. Then you will all return to Piute. As for Sheriff Mulhall—"

"I believe I can persuade Mulhall that Slade Salters is the gent who most requires his attention," Jim told him. He paused then. "But how do I know all this isn't a trick?"

Quan Goon glared at him, turned to Sui Chen and burst out in a wrathy flow of Chinese. Sui Chen answered him quietly. Morningstar fastened his attention on the latter, realizing that that shrewd, farseeing man was beginning to emerge as the most authoritative figure of them all. Carlotta was drawn into the discussion also. Presently they appeared to come to some decision. Carlotta turned to Jim.

"I have offered to remain here while you are waiting for Miss Orme," she said. "Quan Goon and several others will stay too. Will that satisfy you, Jim?"

He did not hesitate over his answer. "You know it will, Carlotta," he assured her.

Darkness was creeping out of the gulches and canyons about the pueblo when Sui Chen and the Chinese made ready to leave. Morningstar's party was given their guns. The yellow men who were remaining eyed them warily. Jim read the meaning of that quickly enough. The Orientals wished to assure themselves that the agreement was being carried out on both sides.

Sui Chen's party left a moment later. Jim watched them disappear in the maze of the ruins. He surprised Carlotta's gaze on him then. She knew he was asking himself why Quan Goon had elected to stay.

"You may put your mind at rest, Jim. Things will be all right," she told him quietly. Morning-star nodded.

They moved apart from the others, and for a time silence held them. Far in the west the last vestiges of the sunset burned, a dying coal, its light concentrated on Pueblo Grande, so that it stood out as if lit by some inner glow; but the rimrock and the nearby draws were all shadowy and vague. Overhead the stars were coming out.

"I was afraid you would not take kindly to my return," Morningstar said at last. "I did what I thought was best for all of us—especially you."

"It is all right, Jim," she murmured. "Your way was the best. I can see it now." She gazed at him, her mysterious eyes dark pools that defied his reading. "A few hours more and we'll be saying good-by, this time for good."

He moved his broad shoulders uncomfortably. Was it wistful regret he found in her tone? He had always seen her in a romantic light. But, somehow, the promise of Jennifer's return—her seeming nearness—left no room in his mind for any other woman.

"Don't say that. I'll be in Reno from time to time. We'll see each other," he asserted, secretly unable to decide whether this was a way of letting her down or if he really meant it. And then: "Shall we join the others?"

Sulphur, Merriam and the punchers had taken possession of the adobe before which so much had happened. Quan Goon watched, wooden faced, as Merriam prowled the room restlessly, taking care not to get too close to them, but eying them from time to time as if he wanted only an excuse for some kind of an outbreak.

"Fer God's sake, Merriam, yuh shore give me the creeps!" Sulphur protested gruffly. "Calm down, can't yuh? There ain't nothin' to do but wait."

Bill flung him some surly response which Jim failed to catch. Merriam whirled toward the latter as he and Carlotta advanced.

"This is a nice fix, Morningstar!" he exclaimed tensely. "How do we know those yellow devils will do as they promised?" He gestured toward Carlotta. "This half-caste girl—a hostage! Do you know how much or little she means to them? What can we do if they conveniently forget all about her?" He flung the questions as if they were unanswerable. "They're well aware that Mulhall will get here sooner or later with his posse! They know Jennifer will tell us everything if she is ever released."

"Miss Orme knows nothing," Quan Goon growled sullenly. "She was blindfolded at the time she was taken away from your camp and has been permitted to see only what we wanted her to."

Merriam would have made a sharp retort, but Morningstar halted him. "That attitude won't get us anywhere," he pointed out thinly. "The least you can do is to keep a civil tongue in your head!"

"I don't mind, Jim," Carlotta assured him, her tone steady. "Naturally Doctor Merriam is worried. We all are. But it will soon be over now."

Merriam chose to drop the matter there. It was just as well, for the nerves of all were frayed and worn thin. It was a hard night. Dawn whitened the east at last, and still Jennifer failed to put in an appearance. Morningstar could not avoid asking himself if something had gone wrong. He was on the point of approaching Carlotta in the matter, when a new thought struck him. Sui Chen and the others were far too shrewd to give them an accurate idea of how far it was to their desert stronghold by going straight to it and returning. A delay was no more than was to be expected.

But noon came and passed, and nothing happened. Even the punchers were beginning to get restless. Finally Sulphur accosted Morningstar, his concern plain in his long-jawed, homely face.

"This is gittin' to be mighty plain readin', Jim!" he declared soberly. "Them gents don't intend to bring Miss Orme back. I move we do somethin' about it!"

"What do you suggest?"

"Wal, we can figure on Mulhall's help. He oughta be gettin' here before long."

Jim shook his head. "Not a chance, Sulphur. Huck couldn't possibly make it inside of two or three more days."

"He couldn't, huh?" the lanky one retorted. "The hell he couldn't—here he comes now!"

He was gazing through the window opening as he spoke. Morningstar shoved up beside him for a hasty look. What he saw made him catch his breath; his lips thinned in a straight line as the truth hit him. Down the draw, half a mile from the pueblo, a large band of horsemen came riding—and there wasn't a Chinese among them.

"That ain't Mulhall!" he cried, tension riding his tone. "It's Salters—Bronc Yeager—the whole damned gang of them! They're coming here!"

Even as he spoke it flashed in his brain that they could slip away undetected. There was still time. The Chinese had secret ways out of the pueblo. Quan Goon knew them. The next instant a thought struck him that drained the blood from his face. If they stole away, and Jennifer were returned, what would happen to her? Salters would ruthlessly drag the secret of the rimrock from her.

"God!" he groaned. "Where can Sui Chen be keeping her? Why don't they come?"

13

Salters and his men drew near rapidly. Watching them, Morningstar realized that they knew what awaited them at the pueblo. Whatever the cost might be, they were obviously bent on retaking Carlotta! Seeing his hand forced, he whirled to find Quan Goon at his back. The Oriental was watching him narrowly. Jim threw quick words at him.

"Those men will be here in a few minutes!" he exclaimed. "It's Salters and his crowd! You know what they want! We've got to get away from here in a hurry!"

Quan returned his look stolidly. If he was conscious of the imminent need for action he failed to show it. His only answer was a shake of the head. Jim flung a look at his men. The Chinese stared at him stubbornly, plainly intent on remaining where they were. One tapped his rifle significantly. "We flight!" he said.

"Something's got to be done, Morningstar!" Bill Merriam burst out, his tone taut. "We can't let Salters find us here. If it means blasting these Chinks out of our way, all right!"

"Hold on!" Jim cut him off sharply. "Salters hasn't got us licked yet. Don't do anything foolish."

"Have you got to have grief rammed down your throat before you can see it?" Merriam hurled at him. "Good God, man! Hell will be popping here—" He choked off the rest at a look from Jim.

Turning his back on him, a glance told Morningstar that the renegades were close to the base of the slope now, casting speculative eyes up toward the pueblo. A few minutes and they would be starting up the trail.

Out of the corner of his eye Jim saw Carlotta speak to Quan Goon hurriedly. She was trying to reason with him. But Quan listened to her rapid-fire Chinese without any sign of interest. At last she turned to Jim.

"He insists on standing his ground, Jim!" she told him. "I can't make him see the utter folly of it. What can be done?"

It was no surprise to Morningstar. He reflected swiftly. "There's only one thing we can do," he answered then. "We'll dig ourselves in and make a stab at standing Salters off!"

Sulphur heard him, and Johnnie and Hap Failes. They nodded approval. Bill Merriam would have protested vehemently, but at a stare from Sulphur he changed his mind.

The next moment all caught a sound which froze them in their tracks. It was a rattle of loose stones from outside, at a distance of not more than a hundred yards.

"Don't make so damned much noise, Curly!"

they heard Slade Salters exclaim harshly. "If they're here in the ruins they won't want much warning to put them on their guard!"

Jim stepped to the window for a guarded look. What he saw held him motionless for a moment. Salters' men had reached the pueblo. They were poking about like beagles. Bronc Yeager, a giant of a man, with a cruel, rudely carved face, was directing the search.

Had there been any hope of lying low and avoiding discovery, Jim would have approved the plan. But Slade's thugs were steadily working closer. Within a matter of minutes they would be here unless something was done to halt them. Answering to impulse, he stepped into plain sight.

"Salters!" he called.

The nearness of the quarry plainly came as a surprise. Salters and his men whirled, venting exclamations. Slade flung up his gun. Morningstar cried: "Go back! We've got you covered, and we'll shoot to kill!" They were brave words.

His answer was a burst of firing. Slugs thudded into the walls, bringing rills of crumbling adobe sifting down. "It's them!" Bronc Yeager shouted. "I'm a hoss thief if we ain't got 'em now!"

Jim flung a shot at the owlhoot and ducked back to cover just as half-a-dozen guns blazed. Even so, a bullet tore through his shirt at the collar. Another grazed his cheek.

Johnnie and Hap Failes had stationed themselves at one of the other windows. When the fusillade was directed at Morningstar they fired. One of Slade's men let out a yell and dived behind a sheltering wall; another dropped his rifle and grabbed his shattered arm.

The rumble of the exchange echoed weirdly through the ruins before silence returned. Salters was obviously sizing up the situation. When Jim stole a look he could see no one. But he knew that desperate crew was there—waiting.

There was this moment of delayed suspense, and then the attorney yelled: "Morningstar!"

Jim didn't answer. He had no desire for a parley with the man. But that did not deter Salters. He raised his voice threateningly: "You know what we're here for, Morningstar! We want that girl and we mean to have her! If you want to get off with your hide shove her through that door— we'll take her and leave without firing another shot!"

Morningstar disdained to respond.

"You haven't got a chance if you try to stand us off!" Slade drove on persuasively. "You're outnumbered and you know it! Do the sensible thing while there's time—ten or fifteen minutes from now may be too late!"

Without warning he received an answer to his ultimatum. It came in the form of a sudden shot which rang out as Sulphur's rifle barked. Salters had unconsciously relaxed his vigilance as he talked. The small portion of his hat which showed above the coping of the thick mud wall, behind which he crouched with Yeager and several others, had been too much for Sulphur Riley.

The besieged were regaled with a savage outburst of cursing as Slade's hat was torn from his head and carried half-a-dozen feet away. "That settles it!" he cried. "Smoke 'em out of there, boys, and don't waste any time doing it! Rush them, and let them have what they're asking for!"

The renegades surged up from cover as if at a prearranged signal. But their charge stalled before it really got started. Morningstar and the others had been waiting for just such an opportunity. The instant the first attacker showed his head around the corner of a wall they unleashed a blast which would have daunted an even larger force.

Bronc Yeager took charge then, the authoritative rasp of his voice bespeaking a callousness and drive unknown to the lawyer.

"Crawl up on 'em, boys!" he barked. "Work around the back of that place! We'll make duck soup of them birds in a hurry, since that's the way they want it!"

Jim, Merriam and the punchers, as well as the Chinese with Quan Goon, had found a vantage point from which to fire whenever a fair target presented itself. It was not often. The renegades were sniping at them from three or four directions.

Morningstar knew this grim struggle could end in only one way now. It was simply a matter of time. He flashed a glance at Carlotta. The girl's poise amazed him. Tense as she knew the situation to be, she showed no sign of cracking.

Catching his eye, she moved to his side, though he motioned her back.

"Jim—let me help!" she pleaded. "I've never fired a gun in my life, but at least I can try!"

"Keep back, Carlotta!" he ordered, his tone gruff and final. "Getting hit won't help us. We'll take care of this!"

His assurance was more for her peace of mind than anything else, however. Even Merriam got that. He growled: "This can't last much longer at the rate it's going, Morningstar."

He was right. So complex was the construction of the pueblo that the attackers steadily drew in, narrowing the net they were drawing about their quarry. Jim had no doubt about what would happen when Yeager decided the time was ripe for the deciding action. His gang would come pouring in, their guns blazing. In a minute or two it would be all over.

Morningstar determined to take matters into his own hands. Attracting Quan Goon's attention, he ordered the man by a sharp gesture to fall back toward the inner door. The Oriental hesitated. But, knowing how desperate their plight was, he nodded woodenly and started to obey. Jim said:

"Follow him, all of you! We've got to squeeze out of this before the pinch gets any tighter! Carlotta, you go with Sulphur and Johnnie!"

She obeyed without demur. The remaining Chinese raised no objection to the move. Morningstar delayed at his window long enough to fire a last shot or two in the hope of deceiving Salters and his crowd for another precious moment. Then he turned and followed.

The door gave on a passage which opened on an inner room. The tiny cubicle was dark except for a faint glow of light from overhead. For an instant Jim was afraid they were trapped and could go no farther; then he saw the crude ladder leading up through a hole in the roof.

"Get up there!" he urged. "And hurry!"

Sulphur went first, wary of ambush. After a moment he called back, "Okay." The others followed as quickly as possible, Carlotta first. Already there was a restless stir among the renegades outside; they had sensed a ruse and were determined to nip it in the bud. Their rush came just as Jim had mounted the ladder and was hauling it up after him. There was a stamp of boots, the crash of a gun in the confined space below and a bellowing voice:

"They're gone! By God, they've give us the slip, boys! Clear out of here an' locate 'em!"

Sulphur found a way of retreat leading over the roofs of the hivelike pueblo. With Jim leading the way, the fugitives had won a hundred yards and were on the point of crossing a wide roof between crumbling adobe walls, when a burst of shots broke out from the rear. They were forced to fall back to the doubtful protection of one of the walls. Morningstar realized they would be safe there only a matter of minutes, for the advantage lay all with Salters' men. Yeager had thrown out several flanking parties which poured in a raking fire from the roofs as they steadily advanced.

Morningstar gave the word to fall back again. But this time it was not in the direction in which they wished to go. Slade's men had cut them off from any commanding position that might have given them an advantage sufficient to outweigh the odds against them. From one place of temporary protection to another they retreated, pushed back relentlessly. The blood-soaked rag that Sulphur had tied around his throat was proof that the enemy's slugs were not all going wide of their mark. One of the Chinese had stoically bound up a hand from which two fingers had been shot away. Merriam was injured too. A welt on his head oozed blood.

"God, Jim—we're cornered!" Sulphur cried hoarsely, cut off by a lethal hail from reaching a thick wall promising safer cover. "We're on the top of this dang mud pile! There ain't nowheres else we kin go!"

It was true. They had been forced up one rickety ladder after another until they had reached the highest level. Below them on every hand the roofs dropped away. Near at hand there were less than half-a-dozen adobe rooms, their roofing gone, the walls tumbling in. Yeager had cleverly maneuvered them into this trap. Morningstar had seen it coming, even while he was powerless to prevent it.

Merriam saw it too. He whirled on Jim. "I left things to you, Morningstar," he raged, "and this is the result! You'll get us all killed!"

"Get hold of yourself," was all the answer he got. "None of us have been killed yet! If I can prevent it we won't be!"

He spoke too quickly, however. A minute later, directing the retreat to a crumbling, three-walled ruin where it seemed their final stand must be made, Morningstar saw to it that Carlotta reached the spot, shielded by his friends. Merriam followed. Jim turned to the Chinese then.

"Run for it, Quan," he directed the latter brusquely. "I'll try to cover you and your men."

The Oriental was in a savage mood. Blood from a torn ear smeared his jacket; there was murder in his flashing eyes. He hesitated, shooting a suspicious look at Morningstar, then jerked a nod. He started for the walls which sheltered Carlotta, his men at his heels. Salters' gang saw them. They poured in a hot fire. Morningstar saw one of the Chinese stumble and go down. Starting to scramble up, he won to his knees, but slumped down again. That he was seriously, perhaps mortally, wounded, Jim didn't question.

Quan Goon saw what had happened. He had almost reached cover. Slugs from the renegades' rifles screamed about him, but he seemed not to notice. Turning, he started for the wounded man. Jim waved him back.

"Get behind that wall, you fool!" he cried. "I'll get him!"

The broad expanse of the roof was a good score of yards in width. The man who had been hit lay near its center. It seemed to Morningstar that he would never reach the spot; yet it was only a few seconds before he was there. Laying hold of the Oriental, he heaved him up. Somehow he got the inert body over his shoulder. He started for cover.

He had nearly reached it when he felt a heavy blow from behind. He came within an inch of measuring his length, just managing to regain his balance and stagger into the protection of the adobe wall. Quan was at his side in a flash.

Together they lowered the wounded man. Their examination was brief. "Afraid he's done for," Jim grunted. "A slug got him at the last minute out there."

Quan Goon nodded. The blow which Jim had felt, thinking at first that he had been struck himself, had been a bullet which hit the man on his back. It had torn a fearful hole, ranging upward through the vitals. Quan didn't need to be told that the man was dead. And yet there was a strange look in his eyes as they met Morningstar's.

"You do this, for one of us?" he got out wonderingly.

"Why not?" Jim countered. "All in the same fix, aren't we?" He couldn't fail to understand what was in Quan's mind. His action in going to the aid of one of his countrymen had come as a shock of surprise to Quan Goon. Plainly some of his opinions of Morningstar were undergoing a change.

A savage blast from the guns hemming them in warned them that their own troubles were far from ended. At Jim's direction they answered fiercely. The three walls of their refuge were reasonably secure, but the open side presented a constant threat. Sulphur and Johnnie were working feverishly, attempting to throw up a barrier out of the crumbled heaps of adobe strewn about. At a word from Quan Goon the Chinese pitched in to help.

It was hopeless, however. Morningstar saw it even before the others did. A stolen glimpse over the wall showed him Bronc Yeager, waving his men around on that side. A bullet knocked Johnnie flat; he scrambled up with a surprised yell, more startled than hurt. A few seconds later Merriam cried hoarsely:

"Good God! To think we had to come to this end! Nothing can save us now!"

Apparently he was right. Salters' men had discovered the weak spot in their defense and were concentrating their fire in that quarter. A second Chinese received a disabling slug in the shoulder. Quan Goon dragged him back. Sulphur and the other punchers crawled from their exposed positions.

"Jim, let me give myself up!" Carlotta burst out. "I can't stay here and see you shot down one after another! Perhaps if I speak to Salters he'll let you go."

"Not a chance," he refused brusquely. "Slade is mighty sure to smoke us out of here in a few minutes more, but he'll have to finish the job before he gets you!"

It would not be long. The renegades were crawling closer every minute. They could be heard calling to one another triumphantly, sure of their conquest.

Carlotta turned to Quan Goon. The latter had overheard her exchange with Morningstar; knowing how desperate their case was, he yet approved Jim's stand. Carlotta spoke to him rapidly in his own tongue. He heard her out, attentive to the end; then he shook a decisive negative. Carlotta had put some proposition up to him, Jim knew; whatever it was, she persisted. It was several minutes before Quan weakened, and then it was only because a hoarse shout and a burst of firing warned of a rush by Salters' men.

They came on the run, their guns flaming. At a cry from Morningstar the besieged poured in a fierce return. For a moment it was hard to say what would happen. Then the renegades broke, scattering to find cover ever nearer to their objective.

Sulphur started to thumb fresh cartridges into his gun, only to stop. He turned a strained face to Morningstar. "Jim, I ain't got half-a-dozen shells left!" he announced. "How are you fixed?"

Morningstar had only a few more himself. Before he could answer, however, Carlotta was at his side.

"Jim, I've been pleading with Quan Goon," she said quickly. "He knows how desperate things are with us! He has consented to take us to safety if only we can find a way back into the lower passages! Can it be done? Can't we fight our way through them—do something to break away?"

Even as he started to frame a regretful answer there was a cry from Happy. The buckaroo had been scraping away at the adobe in an attempt to pile up a breastwork, even after the others gave over; it was plain he had made a discovery of some kind. All stared at him.

Hap crawled over to where Morningstar was. "I uncovered a door or somethin', Jim!" he burst out. "There's a hole over there where I was diggin'—it goes down into the room under us!"

Morningstar lost no time in investigating. What the puncher had said was so. There was a hole leading down into darkness. It was not large, but a minute's digging remedied that. Soon it was big enough to crawl through. Carlotta's tone reflected the relief they felt at this sudden release from the grim predicament of a few moments before.

"This is what I was praying for! You will not forget your promise, Quan?"

Quan Goon hesitated only a moment. And yet, before he could find words for his answer, there came a fusillade from the enemy even more savage and determined than before. Morningstar heard Yeager directing another rush which they could not have hoped to stave off.

"Quick!" Quan exclaimed. "Down that hole, all of you! We haven't a second to spare!"

They obeyed hastily, Carlotta going second only to Johnnie, who had gone first to make sure the drop was a safe one. Morningstar waited until the last with Sulphur. Both were fearful to behold, blackened with powder and smeared with blood and dirt. They took a last shot from cover at the renegades, advancing pell-mell across the near roof, and then Jim whirled.

"Down with you!" he flung at Sulphur. The lanky one dived for the hole and dropped through. Jim almost landed on him, he followed so closely.

"Jim! This way!" he heard Carlotta's urgent call.

Stumbling through a dark passage, they wound this way and that, presently finding themselves in a second room. Here a ladder running through a hole in the floor gave upon a still lower level. Morningstar kept his ear cocked constantly for the first sound of pursuit. It was not long in coming.

He was about to plan out a course of action when Carlotta turned to him, Quan Goon at her side. "You must allow yourself to be blindfolded, Jim," she told him; "you and the others."

Morningstar hesitated, but what he saw in her face assured him there was no trickery here. "Make it fast," he grunted. "Salters ain't so far behind."

He submitted to the kerchief that was slipped over his eyes and knotted at the back of his head. Evidently Sulphur, Merriam and the others were similarly treated. A hand grasped Morningstar's arm and he was led forward.

He felt himself being led interminably through the devious passages of the great pueblo; in fact he had no inkling of it when the way led out of it, though that must have been the case, for the party proceeded for what seemed miles without a halt. They had negotiated several ladders; from the silence and the musty smell in the air Jim judged they were in an underground passage of some kind. He could feel nothing but smooth stone underfoot and the rough walls that he could touch. Then came a series of stone steps. It seemed endless. If Morningstar had striven to preserve some idea of where he was being taken by the use of his sense of direction he would long since have been hopelessly confused.

He could not have told when it was that he first began to sense the change. The stone steps had led up and up till his legs grew weary of climbing and he would have said there could be no point in all the rugged Fortifications as high as this. But at last a halt was made. Morningstar heard Carlotta's voice. She was speaking to someone. There was a measured colloquy in Chinese, then silence. In the midst of it Jim was led forward.

He seemed to know that his friends were no longer with him. For the moment that fact held its own significance. And then he discovered that the air was fresher, keen with the unmistakable smell of water. From a distance came the call of a bird; nearer he caught the rustling of a tree.

A voice fell on his ear which he recognized instantly. It was that of Sui Chen. The Oriental said: "Welcome to Ping-an-shanku, my friend."

A hand whisked the covering from Jim's face. The glaring sunlight blinded him for a moment. Then his eyes focused. Speechless with amazement at what confronted him, he stopped in his tracks. The secret of Wu-tai-shan lay revealed before him. It was incredible! Beyond imagination! His eyes torn wide, staring, he stood there transfixed and stunned.

14

Standing there, gazing at what was nothing less than a hidden paradise, Morningstar's amazement was such that he found it difficult to credit his eyes. He discovered himself on the edge of a valley perhaps ten square miles in extent, ringed in by ragged desert peaks, with a lofty, compact mountain rising in its center. Sui Chen saw him staring at it.

"That is Wu-tai-shan," he said humbly. "To us it means sacred or revered mountain."

Against the grateful green of the valley Wu-tai-shan glowed red under the rays of the afternoon sun. It dwarfed the objects near at hand. There was something ethereal about it.

Morningstar's glance dropped to the cluster of buildings below. The houses were not jammed together after the manner of Western civilization; each was set apart, small, made of adobe and Oriental in design. Flowers grew about them. A silver thread of running water flashed here and there through the pleasing pattern made by a winding, tree-bordered lane. Beyond the tiny stream a temple tower reached skyward. It might have been a mountain village in faraway Shansi Province, in northern China, miraculously dropped down here in the barren wastes of southern Nevada.

"Perhaps you would care to look about," Sui Chen invited courteously. "The gods have smiled on us here. We are proud of what we have accomplished."

They descended into the valley by a winding path. Morningstar's guide led the way through a broad, cultivated area of garden produce, containing vegetables of many varieties, where straw-hatted Chinese worked with primitive hoes, irrigating with a flow of water that seemed inexhaustible. From somewhere up the valley sounded the lowing of cattle. Morningstar saw that he and Sui Chen were approaching the great red sacred mountain.

Seen near at hand, it was even more impressive. High in the air it rose, its upper ramparts unscalable. Out of a riven gorge in its flank poured a steady flow of pure, sweet water. It came from springs hidden deep in the mountain, Sui Chen explained. But for it, this valley would have remained an unlivable inferno.

They went on. Something leaped in Morningstar when, a moment later, he beheld the mouth of a mine tunnel in the face of the mountain. It was high up, the apron formed by the mine tailings presenting a scene of busy activity just now. Jim's brows shot up at sight of the huge, crude arrastra, the primitive milling machine of the ancients: a broad, round stone trough, round and round which heavy weights were dragged by a pair of oxen, crushing the ore thrown in by the bronzed, half-naked Chinese who poured from the mine tunnel in a barefooted, tireless stream.

Later Sui Chen took Morningstar to a small adobe on the outskirts of the village. Opening the split-reed screen, he motioned Jim to enter.

"Consider this your home, my friend."

At Sui Chen's handclap there appeared instantly a gnarled, smiling Chinese.

"This man will care for your wants," Sui Chen told Jim. "His name is Boo Chung. He speaks some English and understands more."

Morningstar was impressed by these marks of consideration, but there were some questions he wanted answered. When the servant withdrew he turned to face Sui Chen.

"The peace and seeming security of your valley have not escaped me, Sui Chen. But I haven't forgotten what happened down at Pueblo Grande. Just how safe are we?"

Something like regret touched the bland Oriental features of the other momentarily. "Who knows?" he answered frankly. "Our secret is known now, Morningstar. You were right; we could not hope to conceal it always. All I can say is that a number of men have tried to find a way into the valley through the years. No one has succeeded."

"Where are you keeping Miss Orme?" Jim

switched the subject. It was a question he had been asking himself ever since his arrival.

"When I came, three days ago, she was confined to her house," was the response. "That was a mistake. She has since had the freedom of the valley."

Morningstar would have been surprised could he have known how his face lighted up with the words. Sui Chen did not miss it. He went on smoothly: "Your other friends are being detained now, but I will see that they are given their liberty. You understand that they must make no attempt to leave the valley. They will be quickly and effectively prevented if they do," he concluded with simple directness.

"I can answer for them," Jim assured him.

Sui Chen left a few minutes later. Morningstar's first concern was to remove the dust and grime of the fight at the pueblo. He found himself reveling in the luxury of a bath. Boo Chung brought him clean linen and then served him with tea and deliciously prepared food. Finished eating, he flung himself in a wicker chair intending only to enjoy a smoke. Wearier than he knew, he was soon asleep. When he opened his eyes the lengthening afternoon shadows shocked him into awareness of the fact that several hours had passed.

Making his way to the garden, he threaded a cool, winding path. Even as he paused to breathe deep of the fragrance of the flowers a laughing voice fell on his ear that sent him whirling around on his heel.

"Jim! You've come!"

It was Jennifer. She advanced with a glad smile, plainly delighted at finding him. She was none the worse for her experience; if anything, she appeared to have been enjoying it. Morningstar gazed at her, finding words difficult, though there was something written in his eyes that she could not fail to understand.

"I'd almost despaired of finding you," he told her simply. If the statement brought the color to her cheeks he didn't appreciate why.

"What do you think of Ping-an-shanku?" she inquired.

"Ping—what?"

" 'Peaceful Valley,' " she translated. "It's the name the Chinese have given this garden spot."

Morningstar laughed. "I hardly know what to make of it," he answered her question. "If it was any pleasanter I'd think I'd awakened in heaven."

She laughed with him, then sobered. "You're not alone, Jim? What of Bill Merriam and the others?" To Morningstar's ear it sounded like an afterthought.

"No, my boys are with me." He went on to explain events since the day she had disappeared from the expedition's base camp at Pueblo Grande, concluding: "When I told them they'd only be in the way Doctor Birdsall and the others returned to Reno—all except Merriam, that is. He couldn't see things my way."

It was dropped negligently. He would have gone on, but she stopped him.

"Do you mean Doctor Merriam came with you—that he's here in the valley now?"

Morningstar nodded. "We're not very friendly." Jennifer met his look gravely. "Merriam and I look at things differently."

"Bill always was impulsive," she murmured.

Jim asked himself if she meant more than the words implied. But that was absurd. He had no reason to believe she was questioning her interest in the man. He told her that, while Merriam and the punchers had entered the valley as prisoners, Sui Chen had promised to release them at once. "Merriam will be looking for you."

He felt on safer ground when the conversation turned to the wonders the Wu-tai-shan Company had worked in this desert valley. He mentioned the mine. She had been there, she said, adding: "The mine and the valley were both discovered at the same time, so I am told."

"How was that?"

"One of the secret entrances leads through a fissure in Wu-tai-shan Mountain," she explained, "and the mine lies in an offshoot. Crossing the desert from Union City, years ago, the Chinese entered a cave, hoping only to hide. They crawled on and on until they found—this. Many were near death. The water saved them. So they conceived the idea of developing and conserving the water and making a home here."

"It was their only chance," he nodded.

"Gardens were planted, homes built, trees brought in. The birds came." She turned to him impulsively. "Jim, the world was well lost for this! These people have been living in peace. They want no trouble. *Must* it come to them?"

He took his time over his answer. "It will if things go on as they are," he said then. "Sui Chen knows it as well as I."

"Sui Chen is our best friend, Jim—yours especially. He has great respect for your intelligence. Sometimes I think that, if we are to escape from the valley at all, it will be through him. . . . Oh, I saw your glance roaming these peaks as I talked," she hastened on, when he would have interrupted. "I know what is in your mind. You will not rest until you have found a way out; you can't bear the thought of this captivity. We all want to get away, of course."

He nodded, impressed by her acuteness where Sui Chen was concerned. "I wouldn't give much for our chances, if anything should happen to Sui Chen—"

"What could happen to him?" she caught him up. Morningstar shrugged, but his tone was uneasy.

"There are two opposing factions at work here. Quan Goon doesn't always approve of our stout friend's ideas. The knowledge that we are all in possession of their secret might drive Quan to any lengths."

Before he could say more a voice broke in on them that swung both around.

"I see you managed to find Miss Orme, Morningstar!"

It was Bill Merriam. Clearly he was incensed at finding them together before he had fairly had time to turn around. In other circumstances Jim would have taken exception to his words, but before he could open his lips Jennifer exclaimed:

"Bill! Then you did get your freedom! We were looking for you—and here you are."

Somewhat mollified, Merriam grumbled: "Damned small freedom, I'd say! We're here, and what are we going to do about it?" He waved his hand in a gesture which included most of the valley. "I don't intend to waste any time hunting a way out of this. There ought to be a pass some-where up there among the peaks that we can get through. If there is I'll find it!"

Morningstar shook his head. "I wouldn't try it if I were you," he advised. "In fact, I've passed my word that none of us would attempt to leave the valley."

Merriam stared at him, arrested. "Let me get this straight," he exclaimed harshly. "Do you mean to say you actually were fool enough to promise such a thing as that?" Something had warned him against challenging Jim on Jennifer's account, but any other excuse would serve as well. In the matter of Jim's unauthorized pledge to their captors he believed he had found it.

"Bill—what are you saying?" Jennifer caught him up. Indignation whitened her cheeks. "From what Jim has told me, it is due solely to him that you got here at all."

"I wish to God we hadn't!" Merriam cried, beside himself. "Even he can't disguise the fact that we're worse off than ever! He got us into this! Why don't he get us out?"

"Hold on, Merriam," Morningstar burst out, taking a step forward. He kept a grip on himself with difficulty. "Your temper's running away with you! I might remind you that that happened before, and it didn't get us anywhere. I don't enjoy this any more than you do, but things can't be done all in a minute!"

Merriam met his flashing eyes for a moment, and his own dropped. The menace in Jim's tone had not escaped him. He began to perceive that he had overstepped.

"Maybe they can't," he muttered, "but I like to know something is going forward." There was more of this, but he was rapidly cooling off. "It isn't fair to Miss Orme to leave things up in the air as they are," was his defense of his outburst. "I'm not thinking of myself."

"It's like you to lay it all at Jennifer's door," Morningstar thought contemptuously. But he said no more.

Merriam's display of temper had one result, however, which none of them could ignore. Any pretense of friendliness while they were held in this desert garden was swept away; even Jennifer's frank enjoyment of Ping-an-shanku had been dampened. Morningstar would have condemned Merriam for that if for nothing else. It seemed criminal to deliberately make things harder for her, since she had no choice but to remain here for the present in any event.

"I suppose Riley and the others were turned loose at the same time you were?" Jim queried, as they paused before the house which had been turned over for his use.

Merriam assented grudgingly. "They're wandering about the valley, I expect."

It was enough to satisfy Jim that Sui Chen had been as good as his word. Jennifer and Merriam left him a moment later. He stood there, looking after them until they disappeared under the trees, a frown creasing his brow.

"Merriam is going to make trouble for us," he thought. While Jennifer had indicated by neither word nor sigh that she would do all in her power to keep Merriam in line, Morningstar's common sense told him that was her full intention. Yet he frankly doubted her ability to get anywhere with the man. Merriam had demonstrated more than once that he was the kind that cracked under strain. And something told Jim that what had gone before was nothing to the test they would all be called on to meet before they saw the outside of this prison valley again.

Dusk fell swiftly behind these towering peaks. Morningstar watched the lamps wink on in the village, then turned to enter his house. Lights awaited him here; it was as though Boo Chung had anticipated his arrival by a matter of seconds and then silently disappeared. Morningstar was reminded of the strange mysteriousness of this valley and the people who lived here; he sensed how impossible it would be to make a move that was not watched by hidden eyes. Little as he had to hide, the thought was far from reassuring.

He had scarcely shut his eyes, it seemed, before dawn whitened the window. And yet during the night his clothing had been pressed and its various rents patched. There was a new silk neckerchief to replace the torn, bloodstained one he had worn in the fight at the pueblo. It came to Jim that all these marks of service could hardly be gratuitous. Obviously some return was expected, but what it could be escaped him.

He was making ready to leave the house when a knock sounded at the door. Boo Chung materialized from one of the back rooms to answer it. Morningstar heard a murmured exchange, and then the servant was bowing before him.

"Sui Chen come see," he announced in his slurred pidgin. "You likee?"

Jim instructed him to show the visitor in. Sui Chen greeted him with a suave smile. "Boo Chung has done his work well?" he inquired solicitously "There is nothing you desire, my friend?"

"I'm very comfortable, Sui Chen," Morningstar assured him, secretly wondering what all this might be leading up to. "Thanks to you."

The Oriental touched politely on several unimportant topics, after the manner of his race, and then paused, his slant, opaque eyes fastened on Jim's face. "I have something to say to you," he began smoothly; "if it will please you to listen?"

Morningstar nodded, concealing something of his keen interest.

"Quan Goon, Moy Quai and I have had a conference," Sui Chen announced. "During it we came to this conclusion in regard to you. We have decided to ask you to join us, be one of our company. We need you, Morningstar. You are strong, wise; you understand things about your own people which we do not. You will help us greatly, and perhaps—who knows?—we may even be able to repay you."

No flicker of eyelash or change of tone revealed the greatness of the honor he believed the offer to be. Amazement and dismay filled Jim while he talked on. This, then, was the price attached to the friendliness shown him!

"You were right from the beginning," Sui Chen told him. "There is only one course open to us. We must gain possession of this land, locate and file on the mine, establish ourselves in the eyes of your law. Your help will be invaluable. In return you will have a home here in the valley, gold, honor, perhaps even love."

He was gazing past the window as he spoke. Morningstar followed his glance. It came as something of a shock to see Carlotta passing down the broad, palm- and cottonwood-bordered road. Again Jim shot a look at Sui Chen, sharper this time. The broad ivory features were an impenetrable mask, but Jim was not deceived. In a flash he guessed the truth. When Sui Chen promised love, if he accepted, it was Carlotta's love that was meant!

Morningstar began: "I—"

"Do not speak at once," Sui Chen cut him off smoothly. "There is plenty of time, my friend. Think over what I have told you, even as we have thought it over. You will be treated fairly here. Happiness awaits you. Do not toss it aside until you are very sure."

"What about my friends?" Jim queried, after a long pause. "They will not want to remain here."

"They mean nothing to us," he was assured. "We will consider your wishes in the matter."

Quietly as it was said, Morningstar knew how much depended on his answer. He nodded slowly.

"I'll think it over," he said.

Sui Chen left a moment later. Jim stood in the door after he was gone, stunned by the offer that had been made him—all but unable to think. The proposition seemed too fantastic to consider even for a moment.

He had found a way to get Jennifer and his friends out of the valley—but at what a cost! Not only must he give up his own life, dedicating it to these Chinese. It meant giving up Jennifer forever, for he knew he would never see her again.

"How can I do it?" he groaned. "How can I go through with it?"

15

Morningstar was still standing where Sui Chen had left him when a harsh whoop of exultation fell on his ears. He recognized Sulphur's voice. Stepping through the door, he found Sulphur Riley, Hap and Johnnie approaching.

"Some diggin's, Jim!" the lanky Irishman greeted. "Dang me if I ever laid eyes on anythin' like it! Why, we been tended an' fussed over an' all but fed with a spoon!" His tone revealed the pleasure he found in the novel situation.

"I know," Jim nodded, thinking of the price of those favors.

"Thought we was in a jack pot till they turned us loose," Hap thrust in. "There's one advantage in bein' together. It 'll give us a chance to git straightened out on what we aim to do—"

He was cut off by Sulphur's boisterous and satirical guffaw.

"Are yuh in yore right mind?" the latter queried. "I know what I'm doin', fer one. I ain't thinkin' of gittin' away. Why, I been lookin' fer somethin' like this fer years! Gimme a nice little China gal an' I'd be willin' to settle down here fer the rest of my life!"

Jim smiled at his exaggeration. Far from being dampened by it, however, Sulphur exclaimed: "Did yuh see that mine the Chinks 've got, Jim? We jest had a look at it." His voice dropped, telling of his awe. "There's a fortune there fer the gent who grabs it!"

"Them springs are somethin' too," Johnnie seconded with enthusiasm. "That water's a gold mine in itself. No wonder Salters is interested."

They were still discussing the wonders of the valley, ten minutes later, when the sound of footsteps whirled Morningstar around. Bill Merriam stood there. His face was darker than ever.

"Here you are," he grunted, as if including

181

them all in his disapproval. "Have you learned anything?"

"No, Merriam, we haven't," was Morningstar's answer. Bill nodded contemptuously.

"I thought not!" He had more to say, his tone so offensive that the punchers stared at him in surprise.

"Jest what 're you doin' about it, Merriam, if yuh don't mind my askin'?" Sulphur interrupted, before Jim could speak. Merriam had his answer ready.

"At least I had my look at these peaks last night and this morning," he told them. "That's more than the rest of you've bothered to do."

"An' did yuh find a pass to crawl over?"

Merriam answered in the negative. "But that won't stop me. The rest of you can stay here as long as you like; I'm getting out, and I'm taking Miss Orme with me! These yellow devils have a number of exits that can be used."

"An' they got 'em guarded!" Sulphur warned flatly. "Yuh won't git far in that direction."

"Perhaps not, if I were as improvident as the rest of you," was the cool retort. "Fortunately I had the good sense to use a little foresight."

To Morningstar's amazement, he guardedly drew a gun from his pocket. How he had come by it was a mystery, for their arms had been taken when they were led into the valley. Jim wondered if he had stolen it.

"Where did you get that, Merriam?" he

demanded sharply. Bill met his look with defiance, pocketing the gun.

"I picked it up down at the pueblo. It was dropped by the Chinese who was killed. I shoved it inside my shirt while no one was looking." Plainly he thought he had been clever. Morningstar thrust out his hand.

"If you've got a lick of sense, Merriam, you'll give me that gun!"

Bill drew back a step. "I'll never give it up!" he cried.

Jim was rapidly growing angry. "If you want to get yourself killed, all right!" he snapped. "But don't run away with the idea that you're going to endanger Miss Orme with your crazy attempts to get out of here."

"I'm sick of your interest in Jennifer Orme, Morningstar!" Merriam flung at him with sudden fury. "It's about time you were put in your place!"

Without warning his fist lashed out. Jim jerked his head aside, narrowly avoiding it. His own blow caught Merriam alongside the jaw, every ounce of his hundred and eighty pounds behind it. Bill went down as if struck by a battering-ram.

Morningstar waited until he rose to his feet, and then he drove in, pumping long looping blows at Merriam's face. Bill blocked them and came back, his big arms flailing heavily. For a moment they fought toe to toe, neither able to gain the advantage. Merriam's fist connected with

Jim's chin and the blow sent him staggering back. He caught his balance just as Merriam rushed. The latter had not expected so prompt a recovery; he was wide open. Again Morningstar struck him on the jaw, and again he fell.

Jim stepped in close, determined to finish this as speedily as possible and take the gun. But he was already too late. Out of the corner of his eye he saw a number of Chinese who had gathered to watch the fight, Quan Goon among them. The big fellow was crowding forward, anxious to miss nothing.

Jim's pounding had slowed Merriam up. Before he won to his knees Happy Failes burst out: "Hold on, you two—unless yuh want Miss Orme to see yuh mixin' it! She's comin' now!"

It was true. Morningstar had a glimpse of Jennifer's approach. But it was Sulphur who jerked Merriam to his feet and gave him a powerful thrust. "Clear out of here, Merriam, before she sees the condition yo're in," he ordered.

Bill didn't need to be told twice. He slipped away, his departure covered by the others. Quan Goon had his slow look at Jim and followed. Jennifer found Morningstar and the punchers discussing an accident which had occurred that morning in the mine. She was not fooled by the ruse. Clearly she caught an undercurrent of strife here.

Finding difficulty in keeping the talk away from Merriam, Jim was relieved when she left them. "Keep an eye on Merriam," he warned the boys. "No telling what that fool will attempt." He had plenty to think about as he wandered off by himself, scarcely aware of where his steps were taking him. Sui Chen's amazing offer was a dead weight on his mind. He knew, if he hesitated over his answer, that pressure would be put on him. "If Merriam kicks over the traces before I've decided there's no telling what 'll happen," he brooded.

It was all an unsolvable tangle, but from it there emerged one clear and uninvolved fact. He had promised himself that he would win Jennifer's freedom—and the only way he could do it was by agreeing to Sui Chen's proposals. Nothing less than his acceptance of this offer of a fellowship in the Wu-tai-shan Company would insure her being returned to Piute, together with the others. Were he to say no, none of them would ever see outside the grim mountain walls of this desert stronghold again. They would be imprisoned, and this time he would be included.

But if he threw in with the Chinese as they wanted, then what? That they needed him was plain. "The day will never come when these people will be safe from attack and persecution," he reflected. "I'll have to be their buffer, do their fighting!" The situation had a grim irony that was not lost on him. Was this to be fate's sardonic way of righting the injustice his father had done these people? The thought was not easily dismissed.

He glanced up to find himself near a high-roofed joss house, its flaring eaves cutting a sharp silhouette against the sky. Passing the door, he glanced inside. His eye fell on a large joss against the wall. A woman knelt in prayer before the image. It was Carlotta. Even as Morningstar saw her she rose slowly and reverently. He would have passed on, but she reached the door before he could get away. Her face lit up at sight of him.

"I have been thinking of you, Jim," she told him. "I meant to see you—if for no other reason because I owe you an explanation."

"There's no explanation due me," he denied. "Sui Chen has told me everything."

Her dark eyes searched his face as if she would read there the answer to her own question. "You would be happy here," she said simply.

Morningstar was in no mood to evade the issue. "Carlotta," he said abruptly, "do you realize that Sui Chen's offer to me includes yourself?"

If he had hoped to catch her off guard he quickly saw his mistake. An inscrutable smile played about her long lips as she met his gaze.

"Do you find me so undesirable, Jim?"

It was a question he had no hesitation in answering, to himself at least. For the right man

Carlotta was unquestionably a pearl of great price. But she was not for him.

"It seems strange that your own wishes have not been consulted in the matter," he pretended to misunderstand her.

"I have never hesitated where the good of all was concerned. I couldn't begin now, Jim."

There was a simple dignity, and even greatness, in the words that claimed his admiration. "If I had your courage, Carlotta, my answer would be easy."

"Then you find it hard?" she caught him up. And before he could speak: "Has your difference with Doctor Merriam anything to do with this?"

"No." For some reason he found it impossible to discuss Merriam. "Doesn't it seem strange that nothing has been heard of Salters and his crowd?" he changed the subject. "Not a gun has popped. I should think you would find this peace nerve-racking."

"Slade Salters is nothing," she answered. "We've little to fear from him. The situation will solve itself, if he persists."

He had no difficulty in guessing what she meant. Not all the members of the Wu-tai-shan Company were here in the valley. There were dozens, scores, of ranch cooks, merchants and others spread over Nevada, each ready at a moment's notice to carry out orders. Were Salters to prove too troublesome, some of their number would not be long in eliminating him, quietly and efficiently.

The girl turned as she spoke, and, following her glance, Morningstar saw Sui Chen approaching. He beamed on them approvingly.

"I have been looking for you, Morningstar."

"Yes?"

"Moy Quai has no doubt told you that tonight is the Feast of the Moon Cake. You and your friends are invited." The Oriental went on to explain the festival in honor of the moon, which, controlling the tides along the coastal provinces of his native country, thus played an important role in the lives of common men. The moon cake, he added further, had to be made after the moon's rising and eaten before it set.

Listening to the details of this ancient custom, Jim wondered how he could ever reconcile himself to the strange beliefs of these people. He did not hesitate over his answer, however.

"We'll be glad to come, Sui Chen."

The latter nodded. "The feast begins when the moon appears on the horizon. Someone will come for you at the proper time."

That evening Morningstar was led to a large adobe obviously set aside for use on gala occasions. He found Jennifer, Merriam, Sulphur and the others waiting. Upward of half-a-hundred sons of China—nearly all there were in the valley—were gathered in the courtyard, and it was plain that on this night they regarded the moon, which presently thrust its silver edge above the eastern peaks, with especial reverence.

A number of tables had been set up inside. Morningstar and the others were grouped together, but if they had expected to be left to themselves they were mistaken. Sui Chen, Carlotta and the Chinese who had shown themselves to be friendly sat with them, and it was Quan Goon and his stern-faced followers who drew apart. As for the moon cake, Jennifer had no hesitation in vowing her appreciation, and Sulphur loudly vowed it to be the best cake he had ever eaten.

Under any other circumstances the evening would have been enjoyable. As the feast drew to a close Morningstar confessed as much to himself, even while taking note of the disappearance of Bill Merriam. "Still sulking probably," was his thought. Merriam had worn a long face all evening; Carlotta, who sat beside him, had had difficulty in extracting a dozen words from him.

Catching Jim's eye, Jennifer smiled. "Now you've a new experience to add to memory," she told him.

Marveling that she could entertain such a thought, he leaned forward, grasping every precious minute of what might prove to be his last evening with her. "You're not worried?" he asked curiously.

"Of course not. I've every confidence in you, Jim."

Word by word, she unconsciously added to the weight bearing down on his spirit. Morningstar opened his lips to speak—and froze, as the clear crack of a gunshot rang across the peaceful silence of the valley. The others heard it. Sui Chen might have been turned to stone. Hap Failes started half out of his chair, exclaiming:

"What was that?"

But Morningstar knew. Merriam! The thought flashed across his mind in a twinkling. There was no time to speak, however. As if impelled from behind, the Chinese sprang to their feet and boiled into the open; for a moment the scene was one of wildest confusion, in which even Sui Chen and Carlotta forgot their guests.

Jim whirled. "Come with me—and stay close," he told Jennifer swiftly. "The rest of you do the same! Hell will break loose if this is what I think it is! We're going to my place!"

They reached the street. Most of the Chinese had disappeared. No one attempted to stop them as they made for Jim's adobe. They were there in a few minutes.

An uproar broke out not far away as they arrived. Morningstar listened intently, then barked: "Get inside."

They were just entering the door when the sound of scattered firing broke on their ears.

"They got him!" Sulphur exclaimed, his tone harsh. "He can't get away from that mob!"

"Who does he mean?" Jennifer asked in perplexity. "What is it, Jim?" A thought struck her then. She gasped. "Not—Bill? He isn't here! Surely he hasn't been doing something foolish?"

She had her answer the next moment. There was a swift crunch of heels on the path and Bill Merriam dashed in, breathless, a look of haunting fear in his eyes. He was waving his gun.

"You've got to help me, Morningstar!" he gasped. "I tried to make a break, and I was seen! I had to shoot one of those yellow devils! They turned me back! They'll tear me to pieces if they get hold of me!"

Before he could say more his pursuers approached with a rush. Jim sprang forward. "Give me that gun!" He tore it from Merriam's grasp, flung it. The gun sailed through the window. Jim whirled as the Chinese appeared in the door, Quan Goon at their head. Glaring murderously at Merriam, he started forward. "We want that man!" he cried.

Merriam burst into a protest of innocence, stark fear riding his voice. Pushing to the fore, Morningstar thrust him back. "Get hold of yourself," he snapped. "I'll take care of this!"

It was plain to him that the men with Quan Goon were deeply aroused. Unbridled fury showed in their flat faces, and their cries were fierce. In that tense moment Jim knew to the last iota what he was up against. These men were in a killing mood and would stop at nothing. Merriam was not the only one in danger. All of them, even Jennifer, might have to pay for his folly.

Whatever the outcome, bloodshed was certain to result. If Merriam were to be rubbed out in an explosion of mob violence, and the matter ended there, it might still make Jennifer's release impossible. It was reason enough to spur Morningstar into doing everything in his power to save the man.

"Get back!" He flung the words at Jennifer, deep anxiety in his tone. "Get in the corner and stay there!"

Already the maddened Orientals were pressing forward. Morningstar flashed a look at Sulphur and the others. That they understood the situation was demonstrated by the fact that they had grouped themselves about Merriam. Jim moved forward to intercept the Chinese. But he was powerless to stem their furious rush. Thrusting him aside, they closed in on the punchers.

Sulphur was hurled back as Quan Goon crashed into him. A second later Johnnie went down when a fist exploded in his face. Hap felt himself picked up by a dozen hands and flung this way and that, helpless. A knife gashed his ribs.

Merriam had gone down in the first rush. He groveled, cowering, too terrified to lift a hand for his own salvation. The only thing that prevented him from being torn to pieces on the spot was the number of men who crowded about him. Shoved from behind, they went down in a struggling, frenzied heap.

Morningstar reached Bill a moment later, tossing the Chinese out of his way like sacks of bran. Yanking Merriam to his feet, he attempted to haul him clear, at the same time calling to the punchers to back his play. It had come with so complete a surprise that it almost succeeded. But there were nearly a score of the attackers; the hope of holding out against them was useless.

Quan Goon closed with Jim, and his steel-wire arms wrapped about him. Others tore Merriam out of his grasp. Sulphur, Hap and Johnnie were dealt with as briefly. Morningstar saw a hard-faced Oriental advance on Jennifer. He choked back the cry that rose to his lips—protest could only make things worse for the girl.

Swiftly the Chinese produced ropes and bound their prisoners. If Morningstar had been con-gratulating himself that, while many guns were in evidence, not a shot had been fired, the thought was small comfort now. These Orientals knew how to finish a man in other ways more to their liking.

At a word from Quan his men started to lead

them out of the adobe. At that moment, however, a hitch occurred. Sui Chen appeared in the door, still other Chinese with him. He was no longer smiling and friendly. A stern dignity touched his face. Morningstar saw Carlotta likewise; had he needed it, one look at her face would have told him how serious the situation was.

"One moment, Quan Goon," Sui Chen said in their own tongue. Quan turned on him fiercely. There were hot words between them. Following the exchange, Morningstar was unable to catch a word of it; but, keenly aware of how much depended on the outcome, he studied anxiously each change of expression in the grim faces of the pair.

Quan Goon's stand was definite. He poured all his fanatical hatred of the Americans into his voice as he stated it: "These dogs of whites have broken trust! They must pay!"

"Be careful of your course," Sui Chen warned him. "We desire Morningstar to join our company nonetheless because this man has shot one of us— nor has our need of him changed. Morningstar is worth half a dozen of Merriam, but one mistake now, Quan Goon, and we will never have him."

Quan still demanded summary vengeance for Merriam's folly. Carlotta was drawn into the argument. Morningstar strove to reassure Jennifer with his eyes, only to find to his amazement that she was bearing up as well as any of them.

"Morningstar had nothing to do with this shooting," Sui Chen pointed out calmly. "He was at the feast with us when it occurred. You yourself saw his fight with Merriam this morning. There is nothing in common between them."

If Quan Goon remained unmoved, sentiment nevertheless swung to Sui Chen, their followers discussing the matter at length, then nodding approval of the latter's words. Sui Chen was quick to grasp his advantage. He indicated Merriam.

"Take that man away—imprison him."

Merriam was led off. At Sui Chen's sign Morningstar and the others were freed. Quan stalked out of the door without a backward look. Jim turned to Sui Chen.

"I'm glad you've seen this sensibly, Sui Chen. But about Merriam—what will be done with him?"

"I wouldn't worry too much about him," was the answer. Sui Chen gave him time to digest it and added: "I think you understand now. We have been kind, Morningstar, but here, there is iron under the velvet. . . . Let this be a warning."

With that he turned away. But if his words sounded cryptic to Jennifer and the buckaroos they were clear enough to Morningstar. He knew Sui Chen was telling him that in his acceptance of the offer that had been made to him lay their last hope.

16

Despite Jim's knowledge that disaster threatened in the event of his delayed decision, a day passed without his having given Sui Chen an answer. It was a day of anxiety and suspense for the whites. They still possessed the freedom of the valley, unmolested, but the very fact that the Chinese ignored them completely was in itself ominous.

That evening Sulphur, Johnnie and Hap came to Jim's house and sidled in, sober of visage. Clearly they had much on their minds. Jim looked them over and drew his own conclusions.

"Well?" he said, when they waited without speaking.

"Jim," Sulphur began, "what's our next move?" There was driving intent in the query, and all three waited for the answer. Jim merely gazed at them speculatively.

"What's on your mind?" he demanded bluntly.

Sulphur grew restless. "Ain't I said?" he jerked out. "Jim—look at it this way. Bill Merriam's been beefed! You know it well's we do. An' yuh know what it means. . . . We can't let it drag along no longer. We got to git Miss Orme outa here!"

Jim's expression said that he had done his own thinking about that.

"Wait a minute," he countered quietly. "Let's take this a point at a time. You boys are pretty sure Merriam is dead, for one. Well, I'm not."

He sounded so confident that they stared at him in surprise. "Why do yuh feel that way?" Johnnie asked.

Morningstar hesitated.

"Yo're holdin' back somethin'," Sulphur seconded. "That business the other night looked mighty queer—Sui Chen turnin' us loose an' all. This is queerer. If yuh know of a reason why they won't finish Merriam, what is it?"

They all waited for the answer. But Morningstar couldn't tell them. He felt sure the Chinese would not risk influencing his decision unfavorably by putting Bill Merriam to death. If there was no other reason for them to hold off that would be enough. But he had said nothing of Sui Chen's offer to anyone save Carlotta and had no inten-tion of airing his troubles now.

"I've got reason to believe they'll spare Merriam," he said slowly, "but I can't tell you what it is." Nothing they could find to say served to move him from that stand. The punchers gave over at length.

"Yuh always was a deep one," Sulphur grumbled. "Reckon there's no use expectin' yuh to change now."

Morningstar spent a sleepless night attempting to find a way out of the maze presented by his

197

problem, and by the time dawn grayed the sky he believed he had hit on a course which would at least offer a bare possibility of success. But before he had finished his breakfast a piece of news reached him which threw all his calculations awry.

It was as he was drinking his tea that he caught the swift stamp of running boots on the path outside. Starting up, ready as he was for the first alarm, he was not more than half out of his chair before the door burst open and Johnnie ran in. That he was a prey to deep excitement could be read in his face.

"Jim!" he cried. "Here's hell to pay! The Chink that Merriam plugged died durin' the night!"

The gravity with which Jim accepted the news attested the seriousness he saw in it. "Are the Chinese stirred up about it?" he queried swiftly.

"Wal, there's been a lot of wailin' goin' on," was the answer. "It woke me an' Sulphur up. We was about ready to do somethin' about it when Quan Goon come along. He told us what it was all about. Shot it into us pretty stiff!"

Jim digested that.

"There's no question but what it changes things considerably," he admitted.

"I reckon it won't be long before Merriam thinks so, anyway," Johnnie seconded grimly. It was precisely what Jim had been thinking. "What 'll yuh do about it?" Johnnie queried.

198

"Just sit tight," Jim answered. "We've got to be ready for whatever happens."

"Mebby yuh know best," Johnnie agreed grudgingly. "It ain't like yuh to stall this way. I can't figger it."

Later in the morning Sulphur and Happy showed up. They put their heads together. Jim could tell them no more than he had told Johnnie. Neither Sui Chen nor any of the other Chinese had come near him or offered any advances. He was not sure just what this signified, but reiterated his advice to stand pat.

"If nothing happens by this afternoon I'll make a move myself," he added. "You can depend on that."

At his suggestion they prudently refrained from wandering at large about the valley. There could be no point in provoking any untoward incident which could be avoided. Jim thought that was the explanation of Jennifer's failure to appear as yet, since she must know what had happened.

The punchers were still at his adobe when, toward noon, strange sounds drew their attention down the broad, tree-lined road. A procession was approaching. There were upwards of two score Chinese in all, and they moved with solemn slowness.

"It's the funeral for the poor devil Merriam killed," Morningstar muttered.

There were several Orientals in the lead, bearing

banners inscribed with Chinese characters. Next came the relatives of the deceased, and it was at these that Jim and the buckaroos gazed longest, with evident astonishment. Their heads were enclosed in bags whose bottoms were drawn snug about the neck; they could see nothing whatever and had perforce to be led by friends. Their muffled wailing could be heard faintly, and they bowed low at intervals as if torn with grief.

Behind the dead man's kin came the rude pine casket, borne on the shoulders of six sphinx-faced pallbearers. Bringing up the rear were the musicians, playing weird strains on their reed instruments: a dirge that sent a shudder up the spines of the whites.

The procession advanced and passed the watchers without a single slanted glance turning in their direction. Somehow the whole proceeding struck Morningstar as ominous, forbidding. He watched till the last musician disappeared inside the door of the temple and then turned to his friends.

"If there's any question of how seriously they take this that settles it," he said. "It looks bad for Merriam. I'm going to demand proof that he is still alive as soon as the funeral is over."

Jim had some difficulty in locating Sui Chen. He succeeded only when he located Boo Chung and demanded to be taken to the man at once. The Oriental could easily have refused and retreated into his shell of stolidity, but he did not. Ten minutes later Morningstar was ushered into Sui Chen's office and told to wait. The head of the Wu-tai-shan Company stepped into the room in a few minutes.

"Well?" he questioned. "Have you reached a decision?"

Sui Chen's usual affability had fled. He met Jim's gaze levelly and expectantly. Jim shook his head.

"I have come for another purpose, Sui Chen."

The latter bowed. Morningstar interpreted this to mean that he would be listened to, at least. He said without evasion:

"My friends and myself are worried about Merriam. They believe he is dead."

"He is not," Sui Chen assured him promptly.

"I don't believe so myself," Jim admitted. "But I must demand some proof."

The Oriental mind read his drift without difficulty. "I can take you to him, if that is your wish."

Morningstar could be as blunt himself. "Suppose we get started then," he said.

Sui Chen led the way across the village and approached a small adobe situated in a grove of cottonwoods. Jim knew it was no accident that several Chinese were in evidence about the place. They started forward but fell back at a sign from Sui Chen. The latter produced a key and unlocked the door. He and Morningstar stepped in.

Bill Merriam, looking disheveled and a little wild, started up from his bed to stare at them.

"Morningstar!" he burst out. "My God, I was wondering when you would come! Get me out of here! I can't stand it—get me out!"

Jim could only shake his head regretfully. "I'm afraid that's impossible," he said. "But keep your chin up. Things may work out to your advantage."

Sui Chen's opaque eyes said that he under-stood the remark even if Bill did not.

Merriam had a lot to say, seeming to be obsessed with the idea that he was at the mercy of mad-men. He had a message for Jennifer, pitiful in its abject despair. Morningstar tried to reassure him, without conspicuous success. Bill had not been allowed to step beyond this one small room since being captured; he was like a caged animal in his restlessness and his gnawing fears.

Jim was secretly relieved when he stepped back out of the place. But he showed nothing of this in his face, turning to Sui Chen as they walked away.

"What will you do with him?" he asked. Sui Chen spread his fat, well-cared-for hands.

"That is for you to say," he suggested with a suaveness that told Jim he held Merriam's fate in his hands. It hinted likewise that an early answer would be welcome. "I thought you understood that thoroughly."

It was with a disturbed mind that Morningstar

took leave of the Oriental a few minutes later. Their meeting had changed nothing. Bill Merriam was still alive, but he had been reasonably sure of that. He had known as well that his answer to Sui Chen spelled death or freedom for Merriam. If Sui Chen had any thought of leniency in his mind his Chinese inscrutability successfully concealed it. Morningstar felt the pinch of his dilemma gradually tightening.

Passing along a shady path on the way to his house, he glanced up to see Jennifer waiting for him.

"Jim, what has come up?" she asked, studying his grave face. "Has the death of this man killed all hope of saving Bill?"

"I wouldn't say so," he answered. "I have just come from seeing him." He conveyed Merriam's message.

"I've been dreadfully worried about him," Jennifer said. "I know his foolishness has made matters infinitely harder for you."

Jim read in the words that her confidence in him was still unshaken. He said quietly:

"I believe I can get you all out of here in a day's time—Merriam included." It was hard to say, but there was little point in delaying longer, he reflected, studying the curving line of her chin and throat. There was only one answer to give Sui Chen.

"My faith in you is such that I believe you can—

however impossible it seems," she said softly, coloring under his scrutiny. "But how, Jim?"

It was the last thing in the world he wanted her to know. "Sui Chen has some confidence in me," he said evasively. "I may be able to persuade him."

She refused to be content with so vague an answer.

"You mean you'd rather not tell me?"

She saw in his dark eyes that it was so. But he said: "I've had a—a business proposition put to me. If I accept I may be of some service to you and the others."

Jennifer's face was suddenly bloodless.

"Jim—what sort of proposition are you referring to?" she demanded breathlessly.

Bit by bit she forced the truth out of him until she was in full possession of it. "You mean that you would consider purchasing our liberty at such a price?" she cried. The fact appalled her. "Jim, you must be mad!" None of his protestations that it was the sensible course made any difference.

"I forbid you to do this monstrous thing!" she protested. "I'd—I'd refuse to leave!" Her tone changed. "At least wait," she pleaded. "You say yourself that playing for time has been no mistake to the present. In fairness to yourself, won't you hold off a little longer? If you won't do it for your own sake, Jim—do it for me! Please!"

What he saw in her eyes warned him that he didn't dare tell her that every hour of delay now only made his decision more certain and harder to face. "I can wait a little longer," he got out with an effort. "And remember—Sulphur and the others are not to know a word of this."

When they parted Jennifer did not return home. Instead, she hurried across the village, her thoughts racing. And they were strange thoughts that filled her mind to overflowing. She had never dreamed that what Jim Morningstar might choose to do could concern her so closely. And yet she knew she loved him. Nothing else mattered. Bill Merriam's cause had always been a lost one. It was without meaning now. Her professional, well-ordered life, with its little successes, seemed equally meaningless. Something infinitely more precious was hers—something she was deter-mined not to lose.

Though occupied as she was with her thoughts, she was not wandering aimlessly. A glimpse of Carlotta, feeding Sui Chen's pheasants, turned her that way.

"Might I have a word with you?" Jennifer asked.

"Of course."

They eyed each other with a distant hostility.

"It's about Jim." Unconsciously Jennifer stabbed the other by her easy use of that name. "He has unwillingly told me of this terrible bargain that has been offered him. He is to buy our release!" She paused, then said bluntly: "Carlotta, I believe that you engineered this affair from the beginning."

Carlotta's smile was coldly inscrutable.

"How can it concern you?" she countered flatly. "Jim Morningstar means nothing to you." Jennifer's cheeks flamed.

"Don't try to evade me," she retorted. "You want this man. This is your way of getting him!"

The smoldering defiance in Carlotta's dark eyes suddenly came to the surface. "And why not? I will take him any way I can get him. Who are you," she demanded, "to raise the question? I thought you were concerned only about Doctor Merriam."

Jennifer rose to the occasion, determined to fight Carlotta on her own terms. "You are quite right," she said, with surprising calm. Doctor Merriam and I are interested only in leaving here as quickly as possible. But I resent being indebted to Jim Morningstar in this fashion. There is no reason why he should make any sacrifice for us."

"To call his acceptance of what we are offering him a sacrifice is a rather strange point of view," Carlotta observed coolly, completely taken in. "As our business agent with the outside world, he will be free to come and go as he pleases, and he will have wealth beyond his dreams. Such faith as we shall repose in him might better be called an honor. If there is any sacrifice entailed it lies in the rather amusing fact that he hesitates over his acceptance because he feels he will be cutting himself off from you, Miss Orme. It seems he imagines himself in love with you."

Jennifer felt her throat tighten. Valiantly she strove to dissemble the excitement the words produced in her.

"That is absurd," she said evenly. "He—he could hardly mean anything to me."

"I should tell him that," Carlotta suggested. "It will make his decision very easy, I assure you."

"I shall tell him," Jennifer answered.

She turned away, her pulses pounding. "I shall tell him," she thought, "but it will be to say that I love him, that I would rather spend my life here than have him barter himself away like this!"

She went to Jim's place at once, only to find he was not there. Boo Chung, Morningstar's servant, finally appeared. From him she learned that Jim had gone to Sui Chen's office. Fearful of what it meant, she hastened there. Jim stepped out as she neared the door. The gravity of his expression did not reassure her.

"Jim—what have you done?" she implored.

"I have accepted Sui Chen's offer," he said soberly. "I have given my word and oath before witnesses."

"Oh, Jim—Jim, why did you do it?" she

entreated, her eyes filling. "You told me you would wait."

"I couldn't wait, Jennifer. It had to be this way. It will be best for us all."

"No, Jim, that isn't why you gave in. You said yes because you love me—because you thought it was the only way I could be returned to my people." Her hands caught his. "Oh, my darling," she whispered. "I can't go—not this way!"

Morningstar could only gaze at her in his surprise, words beyond him for the moment. Before he could speak the door opened behind them. Sui Chen stepped out.

"Miss Orme," he said, "you will be prepared to leave tomorrow for Piute. Doctor Merriam and the other men will accompany you."

17

"Yuh say we're goin' outa here, an' soon?" Sulphur Riley exclaimed. "Wal! I been waitin' to hear that, Jim! There's been more 'n enough desert in my dish to do me fer a while."

Johnnie and Hap agreed. "Reckon it's about time we got back to punchin' cows," said Hap. "I suppose we'll all be driftin' back to Humboldt County, eh, Jim?"

Morningstar shook his head. "I won't be going with you this time, boys. I'm staying here."

"Huh?"

They stared at him, arrested. "What yuh mean yuh won't be goin' with us?" Sulphur demanded suspiciously. "What is there to keep yuh here?"

"Sui Chen has made me a business proposition," Jim told them. "One that's so attractive that I've decided to accept." It was said easily enough and without any hint of what his decision was costing him. But Sulphur continued to study him shrewdly, his long face serious for once.

"Sunthin' funny here," he declared. "Yuh save Merriam's neck an' git us turned loose—but yuh ain't tellin' us nothin'! What's the answer?"

But Morningstar refused to satisfy his curiosity. "The success of the proposition depends on its secrecy," he lied. "All I can say is that what I'm doing is of my own free will. Does that satisfy you?"

Plainly it did not. Sulphur did not take kindly to the idea of leaving this man behind when he went out of the valley. They were still arguing the matter when the ear-filling blast of a conch horn, coming from somewhere across the valley, smote their ears.

They looked their questions at one another. "What do yuh reckon that means?" Sulphur demanded. Before anyone could answer the blast was echoed by another conch, from the village this time. There was a stirring, uneasy quality in the sound.

The next moment Morningstar whirled in time to see a dozen horsemen burst from the edge of the town, Quan Goon at their head. They made for Wu-tai-shan Mountain at a slashing pace.

"Somethin's wrong!" Johnnie exclaimed. "There wouldn't be all this hullabaloo unless it was pretty serious neither!" Jim nodded curtly. He had already seen the Chinese hurrying in from the fields.

Quan Goon and his followers could be seen approaching the mountain. They were taking the trail to the mine. Even as Jim and the others watched they flicked out of sight behind a rocky shoulder. "Somethin' doin' up there, that's shore!" Hap averred.

Sulphur held up his hand warningly a moment later. "Listen!" burst from him in a forceful tone. "Hear that? That's shootin'!"

He was right. Clearly the popping of gunfire came to their ears on the still air. Morningstar was asking himself what it could mean when, without warning, Quan Goon and his men reappeared. This time they were racing away from the mine.

"Now what?" Johnnie grunted tensely.

He had his answer at once. Scarcely had the Chinese cleared the flank of the mountain, in full flight now, before their pursuers appeared. Morningstar saw better than a score of men in that loosely strung-out band, dwarfed by distance, yet clearly discernible for what they were. His jaw dropped.

"White men!" he cried. "Salters! It couldn't be anyone else!"

The sound of firing grew sharper. As if conscious that nothing less than disaster lay in retreat, Quan Goon was making a desperate stand. Even Jim could tell that it was hopeless. Steadily the Chinese were being driven back, despite the fact that others hurried to their support. Suddenly Quan Goon dashed toward the village.

Sulphur and the punchers followed all this alertly. Jim was brought to himself by the sound of running feet near at hand. He turned to see Jennifer approaching.

"What is it, Jim?" she exclaimed breathlessly. "What is happening?"

He was explaining as much as he knew, when he espied Sui Chen and Quan Goon making for him. Carlotta appeared a moment later, but it was to the men that Morningstar turned his attention.

"Morningstar, you are one of us now! You must help!" boiled out of Quan Goon roughly. Sui Chen was more temperate, grave as his mien showed the situation to be.

"Can we count on you?" he asked. Jim's nod was brief.

"Provided I'm given a free hand."

"Of course," Sui Chen said without hesitation, looking at Quan Goon for agreement. Whatever

211

the latter might think of Morningstar, he had a real respect for his fighting ability. He assented curtly.

"It is in your hands," he told Jim.

Morningstar turned to the punchers. "I'll expect you to look after Miss Orme, boys. This is my fight."

"Yeh?" Sulphur tossed back, grinning. "Wal, if it's yores it's ours too—jest give us our guns!"

Jim turned to Jennifer. Carlotta stepped forward and spoke before he could open his lips. "I'll see that Miss Orme is safe," she told him. "You need have no concern for her."

It was all Morningstar wanted. He turned away, accompanied by Sui Chen, Quan Goon and the cowboys. Jennifer stood rooted in her tracks, gazing after them. When she spoke it was to turn on the other girl accusingly.

"You won, Carlotta—and now it has come to this!" she exclaimed, anxiety tearing at her. "Jim Morningstar may be killed as a result of this terrible mistake!"

As for Carlotta, she was strangely undisturbed. "I think you underrate Mr Morningstar's abilities," she answered. "I have every confidence that he will be able to take care of himself." And to herself she added: "He carries the green dragon."

Morningstar's first concern was to find out exactly how matters stood. Salters' renegades were being held at bay momentarily by virtue of a natural advantage in the throw of the ground a quarter mile from the village. The Chinese were fighting desperately. It did not take Jim long to learn that their defense must crumble eventually, however. Even as he arrived he saw a man start up from behind a ledge, drop his rifle and then pitch down. He had been shot through the head. Another was binding up a shoulder wound.

Sui Chen turned to Jim with a hopeless gesture. "They are demons, those men! We can never drive them back!" he cried.

Morningstar didn't bother to answer, swinging to Quan Goon. A plan had already taken shape in his mind. "Order your men to fall back slowly," he directed, above the crack of rifle fire. "I'll take a bunch and drop back to the village at once."

Quan looked his question. Jim told him: "Sui Chen is right: we can't hope to deal with Salters in the open. If we climb the roofs on the edge of town it 'll be a different story!"

Jim and the punchers had been given their guns. Jim picked a number of Chinese who were instructed to follow his bidding. They made for town quickly.

On the edge of the village two flat-topped adobes stood opposite each other. It was as good a place as any to make their stand. "Get up on one of those roofs with half of these men," Morningstar told Sulphur. "Johnnie and Hap and the rest will take the other one!"

His words came with a force and drive that told

the Chinese he knew what he was about. At once his instructions were carried out. "Salters' crowd will be along," he called to his friends. "Wait till they come close—then let 'em have it!"

Sulphur nodded, his head thrust over the edge of the roof. "Jest leave it to us!"

Morningstar hurried back to where the fight was raging. The invaders were advancing steadily, Quan Goon's men falling back as they fired. Jim got a flash of Slade. Bronc Yeager was with him. Jim knew the owlhoot was responsible for whatever success the renegades were having. Throwing his rifle to his shoulder, he flung a shot at Yeager. Smoke drifted out there, the brush obscured his vision. He couldn't tell whether he had made a hit or not. But a moment later he heard Bronc's bull voice urging his men on to fresh efforts.

The invaders rallied to such effect that suddenly the Chinese broke. Morningstar didn't try to hold them. "Get back to the buildings!" he cried.

Quan Goon was still fighting fiercely. He was using a Spencer .56, one of the old-time buffalo guns—a blunderbuss that had found its way into the valley from God knew where. He and Morningstar covered the rear, stubbornly checking the renegades' advance, but retreating steadily in the direction of the adobes.

Jim had lost his hat minutes ago. A slug clipped the hair at the side of his head; another droned off his rifle stock. Oblivious of the danger, he stopped in his tracks to answer hotly. Quan Goon remained at his side, refusing to leave.

Suddenly the stamp of ironshod hoofs fell on their ears. Morningstar knew what that spelled. Salters' men were taking to the horses again, ready to follow the retreating Chinese into the village with a rush.

"Get up on the nearest roof!" Jim flung at Quan. "Hustle!" Seeing the Oriental run for one of the adobes, he headed toward the other. He didn't know whether he had time to make it or not. Salters' crowd was coming; he could hear their cries and the scattered firing.

Leaping to a window sill, he made a grab for the roof's edge. It was too high to reach. Jim's heart sank. If the renegades swept close to find him here in the open, alone, they would mow him down as condemned men were shot against a wall. Already their lead was clipping the leaves near at hand.

Suddenly a voice came to him from above. It was Sulphur's. The lanky one was sprawled on the roof's edge. "Ketch hold of my hands!" he cried. "I'll haul yuh up!"

Reaching up, Morningstar felt a strong grasp close on his wrists. Sulphur heaved. Morningstar got his elbows over the edge. "Okay," he panted. "You were just in time, Sulphur!" Even as he got to his knees he heard a guarded exclamation from the men crouched near at hand.

"Here they come!" someone called warningly.

Jim whirled as Salters and his men swept forward, dogging the Chinese who were retreating into the village, firing at any target that presented itself. Morningstar read in their driving determination that they had seen all there was to see of the mine, knew what they were fighting for. No bloodthirsty pirates of the Yellow Sea had ever found richer booty than these reckless renegades confidently expected to grab.

"Push 'em hard!" Jim heard Yeager's harsh yell. "We'll smoke 'em out like rats!"

Not yet had they sensed the trap into which they were riding. Morningstar's one fear was lest some overanxious defender should tip his hand by firing too soon. "Wait!" he commanded the men with him on this roof. "Let them get right up close! We'll make short work of this!"

The warning came too late, however, for the attackers were not yet fairly caught between the adobes when an excited Oriental fired. Coming from above, it was more than enough to warn Bronc Yeager, cagey as the owlhoot was, what was afoot. Hauling in with a jerk, he bellowed: "Hold on! This is a trap!" The others followed his example, reining up uncertainly. Morningstar got a glimpse of Slade Salters, darting alert glances about.

Jim knew that to delay any longer would be

fatal. He raised his voice sharply: "Let 'em have it, boys!"

The men on both roofs fired almost together, a ragged volley that came as a complete surprise to the invaders. The broncs dropped out from under two of their number as if poleaxed. Another man screamed with the pain of a bullet through his thigh. All were thrown into confusion, consternation written in their faces. The terrified horses got out of control, adding to the bedlam.

If the blast did not create even greater havoc it was only because of the poor marksmanship of the Chinese. It had done its work, however. At a cry from Yeager the renegades wheeled back. Morningstar saw the outlaw delay long enough to haul one of the dismounted men up behind him. He could have drilled Bronc in that moment but withheld the shot. If Sulphur had passed up the same chance it was only because he was having trouble with the bolt of his rifle.

A second, scattered volley was fired into the invaders as they started to draw off. It hastened their retreat. Morningstar sprang to his feet.

"We've got 'em on the run!" he exclaimed. "After them!" He waved to the men across the road.

They dropped from the roofs hurriedly, falling over one another. Quan Goon looked to Jim for instructions, all his doubts of whether the other was equipped to cope with the situation swept away.

"Horses," Morningstar rapped. "And spread your men out, Quan! We mustn't let Salters flank us!"

The horses were not long in coming. Swinging into the saddle, Jim saw to it that Quan mounted his own personal followers. Then he outlined what it was he wanted to do. The plan, briefly, was to draw a net about the invaders and drive them back the way they had come. It would work, if it was boldly carried out.

Turning to his men, Quan spoke to them briefly in crisp Chinese. They nodded woodenly.

"You all savvy?" Morningstar rapped. "Then let's go!" He swept his arm forward.

His bronc leaped to the touch of his heels. Sulphur, Hap and Johnnie came close behind him. They soon found, however, that they would be hard put to it to keep ahead of these fierce Orientals. If they were savage in attack they were terrible in defense of their homes.

At a distance of several hundred yards Morningstar saw Slade. The attorney and his men had hauled up, shielded by the brush and young trees. A second later, sighting the oncoming riders, they blazed away with their rifles. Jim and his men poured forth an answering blast. Jim heard Yeager's aroused cry: "Git back! Keep agoin',I tell yuh! They're too many for us!" The next moment the renegades turned their ponies' heads and raced back up the road leading toward the mine.

"Good work!" Morningstar exclaimed. "Don't let up on them for a second!"

He waved a number of men to one side, directing them to work around the enemy's flank across the fields. Sulphur swung off to see that the order was carried out. But Jim could not have asked for more willing cooperation from the Chinese.

Riding hard, Morningstar attempted to overhaul Salters, slim as the hope appeared to be. Slade saw him coming. He whipped his gun over his shoulder and fired. The bullet screamed past Jim's face. Salters fired again. Each moment Jim expected his pony to fold up under him.

Thoughtlessly he had drawn ahead of the others in his anxiety to call Salters to account. He was recalled to himself sharply when Yeager and his men began to slow up deliberately.

"Jim!" Hap Failes cried. "Come back!"

Just in time Morningstar saw his danger and hauled up. A moment later his men reached him. The renegades were driving on toward the mountain again.

Along the flank of Wu-tai-shan Mountain huge piles of weathered and riven rock lay heaped where the elements had flung them down from the high crags during the years. It was toward this cover that Salters' men were making their way. Once there, Jim knew it would be a different story.

The invaders reached the rocks just as

Morningstar's force burst into the open a hundred yards away. Jim heard Yeager calling harsh instructions. A second later a storm of lead droned out of the rocks.

"Stop!" Jim cried out to his followers. "We won't throw any lives away here!"

He motioned them toward the gullies paralleling the mountain. Two horses were hit before they reached cover; a third screamed, rearing, and pitched down, almost pinning its rider. In the gully Morningstar said: "Close in! We'll come at them from the side!"

He led the way, Sulphur, Hap and Johnnie at his heels. The Orientals followed. They reached the rocks. Sliding out of their saddles, they began to scramble upward. Soon they would be above the raiders.

But Yeager saw the danger before they could get in position. At his command the renegades again fell back. They were working toward the mine. Once there, they would be in a strong position.

Crawling from rock to rock, firing whenever he caught sight of a target, Morningstar advanced cautiously. Salters' crowd was fighting stubbornly, contesting every foot of the way. Reaching a point in the trail like a bottleneck, Morningstar saw that the enemy intended to hold them there if it was possible. Slugs whined off the rocks, making a deathtrap of the opening. But the attackers were not to be delayed. Suddenly a yelling Chinese sprang through and ran for a rock some yards beyond. He made it.

In ten minutes the advance was again in full swing. Dislodged time after time, the renegades retreated slowly up the trail. The mine stood on a shelf several hundred yards up the slope. Boulders surrounded the spot, affording excellent cover. Here Salters clearly intended to make his stand.

Morningstar was trying to figure a way of forcing Slade and his men back into the mine, where they could be pinned effectively, when a calm voice from behind said:

"I knew I was making no mistake when I told myself what to expect from you." Carlotta stood there, self-possessed and cool.

Morningstar frowned swiftly. He was about to order her back sharply when Sulphur Riley gave vent to a harsh cry of surprise. "By Godfrey, what do yuh think of that?" he demanded, striding toward Jim.

"What is it?"

"With Salters there! Who do yuh think they got with 'em? Huck Mulhall!" Sulphur answered his own question. "I jest seen him up there! Damned if that curly wolf ain't got the law behind him!"

A moment later Morningstar got a glimpse of Mulhall, standing on the mine apron. Jim stared, arrested. For the moment he couldn't find a thing to say. Sui Chen, Quan Goon and Carlotta had also recognized the sheriff. What could it mean?

Jim didn't know. But of one thing there was no slightest doubt whatever. This, he reflected grimly, was precisely the kind of situation for which he had been made a member of the Wu-tai-shan Company. Could he meet it?

Catching Carlotta's gaze on him, he surprised a look there which said the problem was squarely up to him.

18

After taking leave of Morningstar in the desert Huck Mulhall had lost no time in returning to Piute. With some difficulty he gathered a posse of a size to suit his desires. There were ten men in the group he swore in: seasoned desert men, ready for anything that chance might bring.

Heavily armed and well mounted, they pulled out of Piute without loss of time. The lawman struck straight toward Pueblo Grande.

He had not anticipated any trouble in contacting Morningstar. But he was wholly unprepared to come upon the camp of better than a dozen men when his posse rode down the draw at the site of the old base camp. These men sprang to their guns with a warning cry, obviously cocked for trouble, but they waited while their leader stepped out to meet the newcomers. It was Slade

Salters. Mulhall's gaunt cheeks snapped taut when he recognized the attorney.

"I was hopin' I'd run acrost you!" he rasped, getting down. Slade confronted him stolidly.

"What for?"

"I'm chargin' yuh with abductin' that girl Carlotta!"

Salters only smiled. "You make it sound pretty bad, Mulhall," he said easily. "Don't run away with any wild ideas. I'm a lawyer. I know how serious such a thing can be—"

"Yuh ain't denyin' that yuh grabbed the girl?" Huck cut across his talk sharply.

"Oh, I took her," Salters acknowledged. He didn't see anything damaging in the admission. "It was my way of saving her life. Her people intend doing away with her, Mulhall. They've got her now. God knows whether she's alive or not."

Mulhall was plainly of no mind to be taken in by a glib story. "That's a likely yarn!" he retorted. "What makes yuh so shore of all this?"

"I tell you I know!" Slade insisted. "There's been a split among the Chinese; they're fighting together. Miss Soong got caught between the factions. . . . I know Chinks," he went on. "I ought to—I've worked for them long enough. They can be ruthless."

He went on to give a circumstantial story which seemed to bear out everything he had said. There was enough sense in it to make Huck hesitate. Listening with an expression of grim doggedness, he struck in then:

"All this don't explain why yuh made so much hell fer me an' my posse at Furnace Creek, shootin' the pants off us! How do yuh explain that, Salters?" His tone said plainly that it couldn't be explained.

"It was dark. We couldn't see who you were. It was all a mistake," Slade responded quickly. "We were afraid it was Morningstar and his Chinks. Naturally we tried to protect Carlotta. They were after her—as I told you, they've got her now."

Mulhall twitched his nostrils suspiciously.

"Mornin'star wasn't with no Chinks when I saw him last!"

Salters pretended surprise. "Then you don't know he's been riding with that crowd of yellow devils? Queer! He's double-crossed you, Sheriff."

Huck stared at him dubiously. "Yo're sayin' so," he grunted. "But it don't make sense!" In a few words he told the story of Jim's experience with the Chinese as it had been given to him.

Slade listened attentively to the end, then shook his head. "Morningstar told you that to throw you off the trail," he declared. "Why should the Chinese give him water for you—when they wanted you out of the way? He's taken you in completely, Mulhall," he concluded positively.

Mulhall had to admit to himself that the attorney's argument hung together. He glanced sharply about the circle of waiting, tensed men in Salters' camp, taking them all in. Every one was a hard case with whom Mulhall had reason to be well acquainted. He gazed longest at Bronc Yeager, pointedly ignoring him on the other side of the fire. Yeager was fortunate in not being wanted at that moment, but he and Huck had locked horns more than once in the past. Mulhall's glance switched back to Slade.

"All this ain't explainin' yore present company," he said flatly. "To be frank, it don't look good to me, Salters."

Slade's laugh was deprecatory. "I had to find help of some kind," he pointed out. "I was pretty sure you'd believe Morningstar before you would me. I turned to men who were willing to listen."

Still Mulhall hesitated, held by his deep-rooted distrust of the lawyer. Slade seemed to read his thought.

"Let's be sensible about this," he proposed smoothly. "Certainly we've a common object here in this desert. Despite your suspicions, I'm still willing to help rescue Carlotta if it's not too late. Why not throw in together and finish the job?" He sounded so reasonable that Huck would have remained wary on that score alone.

"What kin you an' these gents do fer me?" he demanded. Salters threw out a hand.

"Well, I can tell you that Carlotta has been taken to a canyon or valley somewhere back here in the rimrock. One of the boys thinks he's located a way into the place. He's exploring it now. We're waiting for him to come back."

It was cleverly dangled bait, and Mulhall showed every indication of swallowing it. He and Morningstar had discussed the problem of exactly where Jennifer Orme was. Jim had expressed the opinion that the girl was being held in some secret stronghold of the Orientals. Carlotta would be taken to the same place. It all fitted together.

Whether Morningstar had been cleverly hoodwinking him all along or not, one thing was certain: Huck intended to gain an entrance to this hidden sanctuary at the earliest possible moment —and by any means he found necessary.

He said grumpily: "Waitin' ain't my long suit."

Slade congratulated himself secretly at the compliance the words indicated, despite Mulhall's impatience. He knew he was in luck if he could carry the sheriff with him now. He would not only have cleared himself, but he would have the backing of the law in what he proposed doing.

"Nick should be back any time now," he assured Mulhall. "Take it easy till he arrives. There 'll be plenty to do afterward."

Huck decided to take his advice. He and the others had no more than eased their broncs, however, before an exclamation sounded from the camp. All turned to see a man approaching. It was Nick Bevans, one of Yeager's men.

"What did you find, Nick?" Slade threw at him as he came up. The answer was deliberate.

"Wal, I crawled into a cave—a long ways in. Reckon I seen aplenty. We better—" Catching sight of Mulhall, he broke off with a jerk. Salters made a sign of assurance, and after a pause the man went on: "It's okay, Slade? Yuh want me to talk?"

"Sure," Salters nodded. "Mulhall is with us. He's going to help us find the girl."

Bevans told of his discoveries in the rimrock, which made it pretty certain that the way to the stronghold of the Orientals lay open. Mulhall listened long enough to make sure of that. Then he straightened.

"Uh-huh. Wal, I reckon we better git goin'!"

No time was lost in making a start. At Nick's suggestion they left their rolls in camp, but clung to the broncs. They were deep in the rimrock; the trail over which he took them was incredibly rough. In places the ponies had to be led. But when they came to the gaping mouth of a cave Mulhall flatly declined to take his horse any farther.

"Drag a bronc into that hole?" he demanded. "Why, hell! It don't look safe fer a man, let alone a four-legged critter. Not fer mine, Salters! Yuh kin do what yuh please; I'm leavin' my hoss right here."

Instead of arguing Slade seemed rather to favor the idea. "We don't know where this will take us," he said, "and we may not need the horses at all. But we'll take ours, to be on the safe side."

They broke off torches of the meager desert brush and wound down the steep trail to the cave's mouth. A dozen yards inside it was pitch dark. The hoofs of the broncs struck sparks off the stone floor; every sound was magnified hollowly. Bevans led the way. For a hundred yards the going was easy. Then the cave narrowed, several fissures opened off. Here Bevans was obviously at fault.

"Danged if I remember which way I did go," he confessed, "but it was into one of these cracks."

Salters took command then. In the mouth of each crevasse he held up a torch until he located one in which the movement of fresh air was distinct. They pushed on that way.

Half an hour later Slade and Mulhall stopped short on hearing distant shouting, then the muffled sound of a gun being fired. It seemed to come from the rear. Their immediate thought was that they had been cut off. Bronc Yeager set them right, coming up a moment later.

"Some of the boys got lost," he explained. "Git separated in this place, an' it's jest too bad!"

"Wal, find 'em an' don't lose no time about it," Mulhall growled. "All this damned noise ain't helpin' any!"

They waited for an hour before the report reached them that the straying men had been located and straightened out. Their troubles were by no means at an end, however. The going grew steadily rougher. Even Salters began to ask himself whether he had not made a mistake in bringing the horses. Mulhall was rapidly becoming disgusted with the whole business.

"This ain't leadin' us nowheres," he averred. "There must be dozens of these caves in the hills. I tell yuh it's a dang wild-goose chase!" He regretted that he had thrown in with Salters, asking himself whether this was the attorney's means of leading him into a blind alley.

Salters' temper was as short. He was beginning to think the attempt to reach the secret strong-|hold of the Chinese was a failure. He was on the point of proposing that they should turn back, when Bronc Yeager, exploring a fissure at one side, let out a yell.

"Somethin's been goin' on in here," he declared. "There's been men workin' here, that's shore!"

They turned that way. Yeager had not been mistaken. They saw signs of the activity of men. An attempt had been made to clear the loose rubble away from the floor of the cave. Salters pointed to an opening. "Have a look in there," he directed.

One of his men complied. "What the hell!" he cried after a pause. "Take a look at this!"

They pushed forward. Work had been done in the cave, and it looked like mining. Primitive tools lay about; a rock face had been exposed. Slade took one look at it and his eyes bulged.

"Well I'll be damned!" he breathed. "Gold! Look at that vein!"

Staring at that underground jewelry shop, the men grew excited. Salters' eyes glistened with instantly aroused avarice. If the vein was as rich as this here what must it be where the Chinks were doing their mining? He had been right! This was a stake worth anything a man had to do to gain possession.

Tip Slaughter nudged him a moment later. "There yuh are, Slade," he murmured. "The hull works, an' no mistake! But why in hell 'd yuh have to drag Mulhall an' Yeager an' the others in on it?"

The lawyer gave him a warning look. "Keep your mouth shut," he whispered. "We'll get rid of them somehow."

Snap Clanton, listening near at hand, a wolfish look on his hard face, nodded shortly. "We better!" he ground out.

Mulhall approached at the moment. He remembered what Morningstar had said about Indian treasure or a mine and was making his own deductions. "This is all mighty interestin', Salters," he said. "How much did yuh know about it?" His regard was shrewd, speculative.

Taken off his guard, Salters could only take refuge in evasion. "Why—it's as much of a surprise to me as it is to you, Mulhall!"

"Yo're lyin'," Huck told him flatly. "Yuh knew about this mine all the time. Yeager an' his crowd, too, probably. This is what yo're after here—not Carlotta Soong!"

Slade pretended anger. "That kind of talk will get you in trouble someday, Mulhall!" he exclaimed. "I told you the truth."

Mulhall took his measure and grunted. "Wal, arguin' won't git us nowhere. We're goin' on!"

"There must be other entrances to this place," Slade responded unemotionally. "Likely they lead to wherever the Chinks are holed up. We'll have a look."

Tip Slaughter found the passage a moment later. He announced his discovery by suddenly firing his gun. "Here's a bunch of Chinks!" he cried. "I nailed one of 'em! The rest ran."

They thrust forward swiftly. To their chagrin the lead pinched out. They were forced to turn back. Slaughter was confounded. "Them yellow devils come this way—I'd swear it!" he cried. "But where'd they go?"

Ten minutes was lost in solving the puzzle. From a dark corner Clanton cried: "Come on, boys! Here's a hole!"

They crowded through to find themselves in the main tunnel of the mine. Some distance beyond daylight showed. They were making for it when suddenly the opening was darkened by the appearance of better than a dozen Chinese, led by a big fellow with murder in his face. It was Quan Goon and his followers.

Mulhall would have called a halt, but he had no time. Instantly Bronc Yeager threw a gun and blazed away. His men followed suit. The Chinese withstood the blast for as long as they could, answering hotly. Then they turned back.

"Push 'em!" Yeager bellowed. "There's only one way to settle this!"

The Orientals were driven back. At last they seemed to recognize defeat, fleeing rapidly. The invaders followed. From the mine's mouth they saw the Chinese racing away on horses. The miners had already fled. But that was momentarily forgotten in the wonder of the scene which lay spread before them. They had come out on the flank of Wu-tai-shan Mountain, and a large part of Ping-an-shanku, the Peaceful Valley, lay under their astonished gaze.

"Fer Gawd's sake!" Bart Cagle burst out. "What 've we stumbled onto, anyhow?"

Salters knew the answer in a flash. His eye took in the sweeping circle of peaks hemming in the valley, the groves of trees, the glittering stream. Here in one amazing scene was the explanation of the Wu-tai-shan Company.

Surprised as he was by the sight, Mulhall

brought them back to the business at hand with a jerk. "There's their town over there!" he pointed. "Likely they got them girls there. Gimme one of yore broncs, Salters—I'm goin' to find out!"

But Slade showed no intention of complying. "You can't get anywheres down there without a horse," he said swiftly. "Those Chinks will be throwing lead too. You and your posse stick here and make sure no one slips away. We'll go down and herd those Chinks back up here, so you can nab them."

Huck assented grudgingly, knowing it was his own fault that he was afoot. He watched as Slade, Yeager and the others flung into the saddle and raced after the fleeing Chinese. They were on their own now. It was no part of their game to round up these Orientals. Their intention was to shoot them down—wipe them out.

They soon drew up on the retreating Chinese. A running fight ensued, which swept on toward the village.

During the next half-hour Mulhall realized exactly what was happening. He cursed himself for letting Salters give him the slip. "Him an' Yeager are tryin' to wipe out these Chinks!" he stormed. "This ain't nothin' short of murder!"

Suddenly a posseman vented an exclamation. "Salters is comin' back, Huck!" he cried. "He's retreatin'! The Chinks are hard after 'im!"

Mulhall watched grimly as Slade's men were pursued to the very shoulder of the mountain. He followed the fight in the rocks closely.

"Come on, Mulhall!" another posseman exclaimed. "We're goin' down there an' finish this!"

Huck silenced him with a look. "Salters was right," he rasped. "A man ain't got a chance down there without a hoss. We're stayin' right here!"

He stepped farther out on the mine apron, gazing down the slope keenly. It was then that Sulphur Riley spotted him from below. Mulhall saw Morningstar also. His eyes narrowed.

"Morningstar is fightin' with the Chinks all right," he thought, "an' he's doin' a damn good job of it!" Sudden wrath shook him. "If Salters thinks he pulled the wool over my eyes I'll show him his mistake!" Jaws ridged, he promised himself what he would say to the lawyer at the first opportunity.

He was so angry that he forgot his own safety, stepping out as Salters and his crowd fell back toward the mine. Without warning a slug from a rifle in the hands of one of the Chinese tore his hat from his head. Sulphur saw it.

"They almost got Mulhall that time!" he cried warningly to Morningstar.

"Tell your men to stop firing!" Jim commanded Quan Goon.

Quan barked out the order. The crack of guns

died out suddenly. The Orientals could not understand, turning to gaze at Morningstar inquiringly, silently asking themselves if there was some connection between this white man and the mysterious appearance of the sheriff.

There was open suspicion of treachery in the eyes of Quan Goon. Morningstar saw it there and knew what it meant.

"I was brought here, Quan Goon," he said quietly. "I couldn't have found a way in if I'd tried. I had nothing to do with this."

Quan Goon delayed over his answer, but when it came it was spoken in the same quiet tone. "I know you are speaking the truth, Morningstar. What are we to do now?"

"We'll hold our ground," Jim replied. "Beyond that I don't know. We can't fight the law and win."

19

When the firing slacked off until only an occasional popping shot echoed across the valley Morningstar took stock of the situation. With the shot that had sent his hat sailing Mulhall had fallen back; he and his men were out of sight in the mine. Why they were holding off, what they meant to do, were questions reflected even in Sui Chen's eyes.

"They are in possession of our mine," he said, his tone freighted with anxiety. "How can we drive them out?"

"They will never be dislodged," was Jim's answer. "One man could hold that tunnel against all of us." He thought a moment. "Is there any other way into the mine, through the mountain?"

Quan Goon said no. "The way those men came in is the only other entrance." Morningstar shook his head.

"Well, they can't carry the mine away," he said. "We're not beaten yet."

A dozen men had been wounded in the fight, one or two seriously. Jim looked them over. "These men should have immediate attention," he said. "Have you a doctor in the valley?"

"A good one." Sui Chen nodded. "But he is old. The wounded must be taken to the village."

"Miss Orme said she knew something about nursing," Carlotta put in. "She will help us." She turned to Jim. "You should see the doctor yourself, Jim."

Morningstar had received a scalp wound in the fight. He had forgotten it until this minute.

"It's nothing," he assured her. He had no intention of leaving at this critical time. But Quan Goon spoke up.

"You go," he said to Jim. "I will let you know if anything happens."

Unwillingly Morningstar allowed himself to

be persuaded. Carlotta and a number of others helped him remove the wounded to town. A dressing station had been established there. The Chinese doctor was working over the injured.

Jennifer was aiding him. She glanced up as Morningstar stepped in the door, and for a moment she stood frozen, the blood draining away from her face.

"Jim! You've been shot! Why did I ever let you go?"

She hurried to his side, her eyes torn with anxiety for him. Plain to be read in her voice, her manner, how she felt about him! Again Morningstar told himself that this girl was a prize without price.

"I'm all right," he assured her. "It's just a scratch."

Carlotta had entered the door behind him. She stared at Jennifer as the latter dressed his wound, naked tragedy in her eyes. All too plainly she read the truth—knew that Jennifer loved this man. What it spelled for her was equally plain. A sob rose in her throat. Somehow Carlotta choked it down. Abruptly she turned away.

The awkward moment was broken by the arrival of a man who jumped from his horse outside the door and ran in. It was one of Quan Goon's followers.

"Quan say you come," he told Jim. "White

flag at mine. Quan say you know what to do."

Morningstar had been waiting for something like this. He lost no time in getting to his horse. "Don't worry," he told Jennifer, swinging into the saddle. "This will work out all right."

She gave him a smile as he rode away. He had spoken with more confidence than he really felt, however. Making for the mine, he asked himself what Mulhall would have to say.

Arriving a few minutes later, he found Quan Goon and the others waiting for him. Sulphur reached his side as he swung down.

"They're askin' fer a parley up there, Jim," he said. "Yuh kin see 'em wavin' somethin' white. We ain't answered yet."

Morningstar nodded. Stepping forward, he whipped off his shirt, answering the signal from the mine. Sulphur appeared dissatisfied with his decision to agree to the parley. He still clung to Jim's side.

"Hell's goin' to tear loose here before long, Jim!" he warned gloomily. His voice lowered. "Thing fer us to do is to pull out while there's time!"

Morningstar shook his head without hesitation. "No. I gave my word, Sulphur. I aim to stick."

"Reckon that settles it then," the lanky one grumbled.

Suddenly a shout was raised. Others took up the cry. Morningstar saw Hap Failes pointing up the slope. Looking that way, he saw that a man had broken through the end of the line and was running through the rocks and brush, making for the mine trail.

"It's Merriam!" Hap exclaimed. "He's tryin' to reach Mulhall at the mine!"

Morningstar recognized Merriam. He knew in a flash what had happened. With only a single guard left over him, Bill had somehow managed to get away during the excitement. He must have learned that Huck Mulhall was at the mine with Salters and the others. True to his determination to escape from the valley, he was making a mad attempt to join the sheriff.

Jim sprang forward. Hands cupped to mouth, he cried out: "Merriam! Come back! Don't throw your life away!"

Bill heard. He had already reached the trail. He hesitated briefly, looking back, then started on again. Too late to do anything, Morningstar saw one of the men at the mine appear on the apron, rifle in hand. It was Bronc Yeager. Risking a slug from below, he threw the rifle to his shoulder and pumped a shot at Merriam.

Bill could not have avoided the bullet had he tried. It might never have occurred to him that the men he sought to reach would take him for an enemy. As the flat crack of Yeager's rifle echoed against the mountain Merriam stopped. For ten seconds he stood there motionless. Morningstar saw his legs buckle then. He went down, rolled a few feet and lay still, lodged against a rock.

"Got him the first shot!" Sulphur cried. "Bronc Yeager's shore hell with a Winchester!"

"The fool! He could have been saved if he'd kept his head," Jim responded, his mouth drawn tight by the needlessness of it. "I didn't want anything like this to happen." But, aside from what Jennifer would think of Merriam's violent end, he caught himself wondering what Huck Mulhall would make of it.

It would not be long before they learned. Again the white signal flag waved from the mine, and again Jim answered it. A moment later Mulhall came striding down the slope, two of his deputies with him. While they were still some distance away, Mulhall spoke to his men, who stopped. He came on alone. Jim advanced to meet him. "This is a strange role yo're playin' here, Morningstar," the sheriff opened up, his gaze sharp.

"I don't find it any stranger than your own," Jim retorted coolly. "I never would have expected to see you with that crowd, Mulhall." Plainly his tone asked the question he did not voice. Huck chose to ignore it.

"I reckon yuh know yo're buckin' the law in what yo're doin'?" he fired out. Morningstar only shook his head.

"I don't see it that way," he declared. "I doubt if

you've got authority to attack these peaceful people."

Aware that he wasn't getting anywhere, Mulhall exclaimed testily: "We won't argue the matter, Morningstar! I'll jest talk to these Chinks myself."

"I'll do whatever talking is necessary," Jim said. "What do you want?"

"Wal—I want them two girls yuh got here with yuh. The whole country's aroused over Miss Orme's bein' held. I aim to ask her some questions. Where is she?"

His demand was an eventuality which Morningstar had not had time to consider. But he said calmly: "She's in the village, looking after the wounded. I'll send for her."

After a wait of twenty minutes Jennifer appeared. Jim had no opportunity for a word alone with her.

"Miss Orme," Huck began, "I understand yuh was kidnaped an' brought here against yore will. Ain't that a fact?" Eyes fixed on her, he waited for her answer.

Morningstar was afraid she would look at him before she spoke. But her poise was magnificent. "Not at all, Sheriff," she said immediately. "I am here because I want to be."

Mulhall reddened. "Don't lie to me, young woman!" he exploded gruffly. "There's sunthin' queer here—an' I aim to git to the bottom of it!"

Jennifer's amused laugh was genuine. "I have

nothing to conceal from you," she told him. "Just what do you wish to know?"

Mulhall asked a dozen questions, only to be stumped by her answers. His puzzlement was plain in his face.

"Wal, I'll have a talk with Miss Soong," he said. "I was told her life was in danger."

Carlotta had arrived with Jennifer. She stepped forward. "I never was in better health, Sheriff—as you can see for yourself," she said quietly.

"Then yuh don't want to leave with me?"

"I do not. If I were to ask you for anything it would be to leave us to ourselves."

Finding himself cut off at every turn, Huck faced Morningstar once more. "I ain't at all satisfied that yo're so peaceful here," he declared. "This feller Merriam—"

"That was entirely his own doing, Mulhall. In fact," Jim went on grimly, "his death was nothing short of murder! Yeager had no excuse for cutting him down; you have none for backing Bronc. It puts you in the position of pulling the chestnuts out of the fire for as snaky a gent as ever set foot in Nevada." He reminded Mulhall of the mine, adding that Slade Salters had wanted possession of it from the beginning and that Huck was helping him to get it.

Mulhall scowled. "I'm not pullin' no chestnuts out of the fire fer anybody, Morningstar," he retorted. "I got in this place the only way I could, but I'm still doin' my own thinkin'! As for the mine, I'm in possession myself, an' I aim to stay in possession till somebody can prove legal ownership to it! I'll bet my soul it was never recorded. Yuh can forget about any warrant of search or seizure," he continued doggedly. "There's a riot here—unlawful assembly. You people are goin' to lay down yore guns an' answer my questions. An' you'll do it peaceably or you'll be forced to!"

Jim shook his head. "You'll never get away with it, Mulhall. Not with that bunch of renegades and blacklegs behind you. You'll have to get rid of them before you can talk to us."

Mulhall snorted: "Is that yore final answer?"

"It is."

"Wal, I'll give yuh till this time tomorrow to change yore minds. Better think it over careful, Morningstar!" With that Huck started back up the trail. He had taken a firm tone throughout, but he was far less sure of his ground than he chose to appear.

Reaching the mine, his first thought was of Salters. The attorney was nowhere about.

"Where is Salters?" Huck tossed at Tip Slaughter.

"Wal, he ain't here, Mulhall," the renegade answered coolly and flatly.

"What yuh mean he ain't here?"

"He's gone, that's all."

For a moment Mulhall glared. "So Salters is gone, huh?" The lightning thought flashed in his mind: "Reckon I know where! Right now he's streakin' it fer Piute to file on this mine, damn his rotten soul!" His wrath blazed up to think that the lawyer had been a step ahead of him at every turn.

It didn't take him long deciding what to do about it. Ignoring Yeager, who eyed him warily, he spoke in an aside to one of his deputies.

"Tell the boys to git ready fer a play," he muttered. "We're roundin' up this crowd of Salters' before they give us the slip!"

The word spread quietly. The possemen took their positions and waited. Huck moved over to confront Yeager. Suddenly his gun was in his hand.

"Hoist 'em, Bronc!" he rasped. "You've played yore last card in this game!"

Barely in time to save his life, Yeager arrested the impulse to go for his gun. There was black anger in his craggy visage as he raised his hands slowly.

"I reckon yore hand takes the pot, Mulhall," he said stonily.

His men, as well as Salters', had been taken by surprise. At Huck's direction they were disarmed. Mulhall looked them over narrowly.

"Okay, start 'em off," he grunted to his men. "We'll hold 'em in one of them side tunnels. If they make a break let 'em have it!"

20

A deeper sobriety settled on Morningstar's face as he watched Huck Mulhall striding back to the mine. He could dismiss much of what Huck had said, but he could not forget his reference to the mine. The longer he considered the matter, the more tragically important it became.

"This passes belief," he declared. "I don't suppose it has ever happened before—a producing mine, of great value, and under the laws of this state really belonging to no one. Waiting to drop into the basket of the first rascal who is unscrupulous enough to grab it! And the law will help him do it!"

He did not have to glance at the faces of Sui Chen, Quan Goon and Carlotta to know that they viewed the situation just as seriously as he.

"We'll die fighting for it!" Quan Goon said fiercely.

Jim shook his head. "No, Quan, guns are all right in their way, but guns will not save the mine for you. White man's law is the only thing that will do it. Without it you are lost. Even this fertile valley will be overrun with white men. You'll be forced out—beaten. This land is all in the public domain. It could have been acquired for a song.

But you have never homesteaded it. Not an inch of Ping-an-shanku belongs to you legally. As for the mine—it's not only unrecorded, but you never paid taxes on it as a property nor on the gold it has produced. Carlotta, you must have known what the situation was."

"We all knew, Jim. But we were afraid our secret would be discovered. Nothing else made us so helpless."

Sui Chen's round face sagged with the weight of his anxiety. "I suggest that we go to my office at once and discuss this fully," he urged. He gave orders that he was to be kept informed of every move the enemy made.

It was a strange conference that Morningstar found himself a party to. From his safe Sui Chen produced a plat of the mine and the necessary papers for filing.

"They were prepared some years ago and never used," he explained regretfully. Morningstar found them in order. His decision was made and he spoke plainly.

"What about citizenship?" he inquired. "How many of you are citizens of the United States?"

"We are all citizens, Morningstar," Sui Chen answered him. "Those of us who were not born in Nevada or on the Coast entered the country before the Chinese Exclusion Act became a law. We have our papers."

"Good," said Jim. "I will not need them, but

you will when you file your homesteads. But that can wait a few days. You have lived on the land and have a squatter's right to it, at least. But the mine can't wait. These papers must be filed at once—before that jackal Salters rushes to Piute and files ahead of you. The county will bring suit against you for the back taxes, and there will be penalties."

"We have no desire to do otherwise," said Sui Chen. "All we ask is to keep Ping-an-shanku and our mine."

"Believe me, I won't stop until I know they are yours!" Morningstar got out tensely. "I am not saying it because you have made me a member of the Wu-tai-shan Company. I know what you have done here, how you have worked. I know you asked nothing but to be left alone, that you meant harm to no one. . . . Well, I gave you my word that I would work in your behalf. I propose to go the whole way. . . . I'm leaving for Piute immediately."

"You won't go alone?" Quan Goon asked gravely.

"Sulphur will go with me. We'll need good horses."

"The best horses in the valley will be yours," Quan told him. "You'll need food and water. They will be ready." He turned to Carlotta. "Moy Quai, I was not pleased when I found that you had included this man in the brotherhood of the dragon. I see now that there was great wisdom in you. This man is truly our friend. May the bones of my ancestors never rest in peace if I doubt you again."

It was a moment pregnant with meaning for all. Morningstar had them affix their signatures to the documents. He left them then to hurriedly acquaint Jennifer with his mission. "I will be back as quickly as it can be arranged," he told her. "In the meantime, I know no harm will be permitted to come to you." And then: "If you care to address a letter to Doctor Birdsall I will mail it in Piute—though I expect you will have been released and be well on your way to Reno by the time he receives it."

"Then why bother?" Jennifer queried. His unexpected reference to Dr Birdsall struck her as strange. She studied Morningstar for a long moment, then shook her head in amused reproof. "Jim, there isn't an ounce of subterfuge in you. Let's be frank. There's something you want me to say to Doctor Birdsall."

Morningstar could only admit the truth. "What about the Flagler expedition?" he asked. "Its work was far from finished. . . . Will Doctor Birdsall make another attempt at Pueblo Grande?"

"Certainly not this year, Jim. The funds allotted by Flagler Foundation must be exhausted by now. But someone will finish the work some-day. That's inevitable."

Jim nodded. "I am concerned only about the

next few weeks. Changes are going to come so quickly that in a few months the Wu-tai-shan Company will have no further interest in Pueblo Grande."

Sulphur had been sent for. Morningstar found him waiting on returning to the office. They set off at once. Since Mulhall was holding the only other entrance to the valley, they had perforce to leave the same way they had entered, by means of the tunnel which led down to Pueblo Grande.

Quan Goon acted as their guide. Even without blindfolds, that long subterranean passage was not easy to follow. At last, leading their broncs, they came out at the pueblo and once more beheld the sun glaring on the vast empty Amargosa Desert.

Morningstar and Sulphur Riley lost no time in getting started. They saw no one, striking out toward the north. And yet, before the peaks of the Fortifications dropped behind them, Sulphur jerked out: "Come on, push that bronc! Salters may be shovin' the miles behind him too!"

Jim so far agreed that when night fell he said they would go on. The late moon was beginning to sink in the west when they pulled up for an hour to rest the horses. Morning found them driving on again.

By midday a mirage rose out of the heat veils. Morningstar knew it presaged the weather-beaten buildings of Piute. The town was still half-a-dozen miles away. One by one they were put behind, until the county seat drew near. For the past hour Jim had been scanning the bleak, brush-studded land about them. But there was no glimpse to be had of any living thing besides themselves.

Sulphur followed his thought accurately enough. He pulled his pony down to a walk. "Hell, we been foolin' ourselves plenty!" he growled. "Likely Salters ain't even thinkin' of headin' for Piute yet."

"Don't fool yourself," Jim told him shortly. "We may be too late as it is. Salters has had a long time to think about this. If he's thought it through to the end we may find him standing on the courthouse steps when we get there, ready to give us the horse laugh!"

Even as he spoke Sulphur was gazing off across the sandy wastes, his attention fixed. "What's that?" he demanded. "Over there, half a mile beyond the second reef of rocks?"

Morningstar looked where he pointed. Far across the flats they saw a ball of dust moving rapidly in the direction of town. It could only be made by some horseman.

"That don't look so good," Jim muttered. "We'll just make sure!"

They swung that way. Reaching a high level, they got a better view. After a moment the dust thinned. They had a glimpse of a man hurrying toward Piute. Morningstar's mouth drew into a thin line. There could be only one answer. It was Slade Salters, racing to town in an attempt to beat them to the recorder's office!

"Throw the steel into that bronc!" Jim gritted. "He's not beating us out now!"

Gradually they drew near Salters. For a mile the three horses raced neck and neck, a few hundred yards separating them. The attorney glanced across from time to time, his face inscrutable; for the rest, he was occupied with the task of getting the utmost speed out of his mount. Piute was in sight now. Morningstar gave his attention to the ground underfoot. A moment later Sulphur burst out:

"Jim, why be foolish about this? Dammit all, a slug will stop that gent in a hurry!"

He started to draw his gun. Morningstar warned him to forget it.

"You can't shoot a man down like that! We'd never get away with it!"

Piute was not more than a quarter mile distant now. The horses were laboring as a result of this final spurt. They were approaching the head of the main street, the issue in doubt as yet. Salters angled in for the same objective. There was a wolfish look on his visage as he stared at them. He would have used a gun had he dared; the same consideration stopped him that had given Jim pause.

Putting on a burst of speed, they reached the

head of the street together. The first houses flashed by. Sulphur was riding beside Salters. For a moment they raced thigh to thigh.

"Damn you, Salters!" Sulphur taunted him. "You'll never make it! Yore bronc ain't good enough!"

Salters showed him a face twisted with fury. Suddenly, unable to control himself, he lashed at the puncher with his romal.

Sulphur threw up a guarding arm. But the blow never reached him, the quirt falling across his horse's withers. Without warning the bronc's stride broke. Lurching sidewise, it crashed into Salters' mount. Too late Slade attempted to avert an accident. His frantic cursing did no good. The next instant horses and men brought up in the dust in a confused tangle.

Morningstar saw that much. He waited for no more. The courthouse was close now. Hauling up before it, he slid to the ground and hurried inside.

His papers were out as he approached the counter. He threw them down and called the clerk's attention. The man nodded. When he took his time about getting around to him Morningstar let out a blast that brought results.

While the clerk was consulting the county records and studying the papers Jim threw a glance over his shoulder at the door. Salters had not yet put in an appearance, but at any moment he was certain to come blustering in. Knowing how desperate he was, Morningstar fully expected to find himself with a gun fight on his hands.

But even if Salters did not go for a gun there were other ways in which he might cause trouble. If he were to swear that he had been delayed by design, that the collision in the street which had brought his horse tumbling into the dust was deliberate, there was a good chance that he might void, or at least delay, Jim's recording of the mine.

There was no hitch, however. When Morningstar turned once more toward the door the mine in far Ping-an-shanku was legally located and recorded, the unquestionable property of the Wu-tai-shan Company.

At the door he met Salters in the act of entering. The attorney gave him an ugly glare. "You think you've gotten away with something, Morningstar, but I'll show you your mistake!" he burst out furiously.

Jim scrutinized him. "Help yourself, Salters!" he challenged.

Slade choked, the cords of his neck standing out. Angry blood congested his features. In that moment he was close to murder. But he was not so far gone that he was unaware of Sulphur, standing a few feet behind him, a hand on his gun butt.

"You'll pay for this, Morningstar!" he exclaimed, his voice shaking with rage. He stamped away.

Jim stared after him thoughtfully. Seeing it, Sulphur grunted: "Don't pay no attention to what he says."

"There's something else on my mind," was the answer. "Wait for me, Sulphur. I've got another errand here in the courthouse."

Turning back inside, Jim made for a door marked District Attorney. A clerk looked up from his desk as he entered.

"Is the D.A. in?"

The clerk nodded. "Just a minute." He disappeared in an inner office, to return shortly. "Mr Hollister will see you."

Morningstar stepped in. A stalwart, square-faced man glanced at him across the papers littering his desk. "You wish to see me?" he asked. Jim nodded. He introduced himself.

"I've quite a story to tell you," he began. He plunged into the strange story of Ping-an-shanku, the Peaceful Valley. Nor did he spare Slade Salters' part in the tale, beginning from the time the Flagler expedition had been turned back and continuing on to the present hour.

Hollister listened attentively, with scarcely a change in his rugged face. He knew Salters and evinced no surprise at the attorney's attempt to grab the mine.

"The Chinese are wrong on a number of counts," Jim pursued as he summed up the situation. "I've told them so, and they stand ready to make reparation. There 'll be the back taxes and penalties on the gold that's been taken out of the mine. It should prove a bonanza for the county."

Hollister nodded.

"Sheriff Mulhall is up there in the valley now," Jim told him. "I don't know what may have happened since I left or whether we were within our rights. Mr District Attorney, I want you to go out there with me and help us settle this matter fairly and squarely for all concerned. Will you do that?" He waited for his answer.

Hollister scratched his jaw thoughtfully. "It's an unusual story, Morningstar," he remarked, finally. "I find your part in it rather strange in a white man."

"A square deal is all I'm asking for these people," Jim hastened to reply. "I have no interest in the matter other than that."

Hollister rose. "If you'll give me fifteen minutes," he said with his customary decision, "I'll be ready to start."

He was as good as his word. Waiting before the courthouse with fresh horses, Jim and Sulphur were not delayed long before Hollister emerged. Jogging out of town, they headed south. Sulphur turned for a last look at the street.

"Reckon I ain't sorry to put Piute behind," he confessed. "I was afraid Salters'd try some game 'fore we got away. Wouldn't put it past that sidewinder to shove a slug in our ribs if he thought he could git away with it!"

"He knows when he's beaten," was Jim's reply. "I imagine he's seen the light and given up."

But Slade hadn't given up. It would have interested them no little could they have seen the skulking figure which trailed them at a safe distance until they pulled up for the night and then took up the watch again the following morning when they pushed on.

That day was an endless boredom of desert travel, with its heat and sun glare. Its one gain was that Hollister took advantage of the opportunity to extract all the knowledge Morningstar possessed concerning the status of the Chinese.

Toward evening the trio came within striking distance of the rimrock flanking the Fortifications. They had followed a winding canyon for a mile and were about to tackle the rugged slope leading up to the pueblo when, without warning, a rifle cracked from a nearby ledge and a slug kicked up the dust ahead of Morningstar. His gun came out and he replied in a flash; they heard the rasp of boots as the killer turned to flee.

"It's Salters!" Jim rasped. "After him! He won't get away with this!"

With Hollister joining the chase, they took after Slade. But the lawyer had been ready for this. Crossing the ledge, they saw him pounding away on his bronc, lying low over the animal's withers and jamming the steel home.

Sulphur threw a slug after him. It screamed off a rock at Salters' side. Then the boulders and outcroppings hid him. Hard as they pressed their mounts, they were able to gain but little. Morningstar was studying the throw of the rocky slope. Suddenly he whipped out: "Swing around to the left! We can corner him if we play our hand right!"

They did as he directed. Once Salters fired at them from an undetermined point, but as they drew in, thinking they had him hemmed in an angle of the mountain's shoulder, they suddenly could find no trace of him.

"Don't tell me he's slipped away in spite of us?" Sulphur exploded disgustedly.

That, it appeared, was precisely what Salters had done. A few minutes later Morningstar exclaimed: "There's his bronc, but he's gone! He's taken to the rocks!"

They were soon at the spot. There were no tracks to be followed; the ground here was like flint. Jim said: "He can't be far."

But though they narrowed the possibility of a man's hiding down to an area of a few hundred yards, and then to nothing, Salters was nowhere to be found.

"Where in hell could he 'a' gone?" Sulphur burst out. "It jest don't make sense!"

"Yes, it does," Jim corrected. "Salters and his

crowd know a way into the valley through the mine. That's probably where he has disappeared—into the cave leading that way."

As for themselves, they were lost in a maze of broken granite and malpais. There was nothing to be done but turn back to the only way Jim knew into the valley.

21

There was a guard stationed at the hidden trail into the valley through Pueblo Grande. After a moment's hesitation, during which the district attorney was carefully scrutinized, the man stepped aside and motioned them on.

"The place appears to be well guarded," Hollister commented tersely.

"These people have found out from bitter experience that it had to be that way," Jim observed.

Forty minutes later they emerged into the valley. Hollister caught his breath at the sight which lay spread before him. Men saw them coming; several ran forward to take their horses. Slapping the dust of the desert from their clothes, they went on to Sui Chen's office. Morningstar found the latter, Quan Goon, Carlotta and several others gathered there. Sui Chen himself met them at the door.

Jim introduced Hollister. Sui Chen's surprise was obvious, but he covered it quickly. "You are welcome," he assured him.

"I have asked Mr Hollister here as the best and quickest way of ironing out your affairs," Morningstar told the Chinese. "I can report complete success in Piute," he continued. "The mine has been properly located and filed." His story of how Sulphur and he had bested Salters evoked a shout of triumph led by Johnnie and Hap Failes. The Chinese crowding around understood in a flash.

As soon as he could make himself heard Jim asked: "What has Mulhall been doing, Quan?" Carlotta answered him.

"He came down the mountain with various demands," she said. "We told him you had gone to Piute—that nothing could be done before your return. He needed food, which we gave. . . . He returned to the mine and is still there, waiting."

"What about Salters' men—and Yeager's bunch?"

"We've seen nothing of them since you left, Jim. Mulhall refused to be drawn out about them."

"Better send a messenger up there. Tell Mulhall to come down right away," Hollister advised.

It was quickly arranged, Quan Goon starting for the mine without delay. Morningstar was asking himself where Jennifer might be, hungering for a sight of her. She had not yet appeared when Quan ushered Huck Mulhall into the office.

Presently the district attorney was presiding over an impromptu court. From beginning to end the affairs of the Chinese company were gone into thoroughly; point after point was ironed out and settled; the possession of the luxuriant valley, the right of the Chinese to carry on here and similar matters receiving full attention. When it was done, late that evening, Jim had the satisfaction of knowing that he had fought a winning fight for these people.

It meant that when Mulhall, Hollister and the other whites departed for Piute Jennifer Orme would go with them. Morningstar could find only a bitter pleasure in the fact, knowing as he did that he might never lay eyes on her again.

Carlotta must have read his thought in his glum expression. Whatever her reaction, she got up abruptly, and, excusing herself, left the men to complete the final details. Jim asked himself whether it was suffering that he read in her ivory-pale face as she slipped out, avoiding his look.

Ten minutes later there came a shout from outside the house which jerked them all up sharply. Mulhall came to his feet. "Am I gittin' jumpy?" he rasped. "What was that?" Morningstar had told him of Salters' bushwhack attempt and escape into the rocks, and Huck had not forgotten.

Boots stamped on the veranda; the door was ripped open. Sulphur Riley burst into the room, his excitement plain.

"It's Salters an' his lobos!" he cried. "They've busted through the mine an' got loose in the valley! They're ridin' hell-bent!"

Mulhall let out a wrathy roar. "Why, I've had Slaughter an' Yeager an' the bunch of 'em disarmed an' penned up for three, four days! I don't git this!"

"It's all plain reading, Huck," Morningstar told him. "Salters came through the mine and got the jump on your boys. He evidently turned the tables in a hurry. It's your possemen who are penned up now. Talk won't help." He started for the door. "We'll finish the job this time," he jerked over his shoulder.

There was a brief delay of preparation. Whites and Chinese swung into action then. Almost before they had succeeded in finding mounts gunfire broke out on the edge of town.

"They're over west!" Jim exclaimed. "We'll spread out and work that way—drive 'em into the open!"

The village was so rambling as to make a clean-cut plan of action almost impossible, however. There were a hundred byways and winding paths to confuse and mislead. Dusk had fallen; under the profusion of trees the shadows were black. Racing toward the point from which the firing had come, Jim was suddenly taken back when a crashing fusillade exploded at him from a distance of forty yards. He answered hotly, heard the curse of a harsh voice, the pound of boots. Shoving that way with Johnnie Landers at his heels, he found nothing.

A few minutes later his bronc shied at something on the ground. Morningstar caught back his shot in time, leaned down to peer. What he saw sent a cold chill over him. There was a man lying there on the ground, and the man was dead. It was one of the Chinese. Jim's mouth tightened. He scarcely needed to be told that Salters' gang was in grim earnest.

At a cry from the left, which he recognized as Sulphur's, he wheeled that way. Before he reached the tiny square where two roads intersected there was an outburst of firing. He got there in time to see better than half-a-dozen renegades trying desperately to break through a wall of fiercely silent Chinese hemming them in. Muzzle bursts freckled the night wickedly with tongues of red. Jim thought he spotted Bronc Yeager. He started for him.

Yeager saw him coming. "No yuh don't, Mornin'star!" Bronc rifled harshly. His gun spat at almost point-blank range, the slug lightly brushing Jim's ribs. Jim fired just as the owlhoot reared his bronc. The bullet smacked solidly against the animal's chest. For a second Jim thought it had plowed on through, that Yeager was wounded. But even as the pony screamed and went down Bronc was hauled up behind one of his friends. They raced off into the shadows.

Johnnie Landers started after them. Yeager saw that. Twisting back, he fired once. Johnnie went out of the hull as if hit with a club. Jim was at his side in a second.

"Did he get you, Johnnie?" he demanded. "Are you hit bad?"

Landers struggled up, sheepish. "Hell, no!" he exclaimed. "The slug must've smacked me square in the belt buckle. I'm sore as all get out, but I ain't got a scratch!"

Morningstar helped him into the saddle. A moment later he got a flash of Mulhall. Huck and the district attorney were busily engaged in routing a renegade from the corner of a house in which the paper lanterns still burned serenely, in fantastic contrast to the violence which had come like a lightning bolt. Huck ordered the man to throw down his gun in the name of the law. His answer was a savage burst of shots. Jim heard Sulphur's whipped-out exclamation:

"They've worked around us, over to the right! They're right into town now!"

Scattered firing could be heard from that direction, above an occasional high-pitched

263

Chinese yell which might have meant either anguish or defiance. But Jim found something on his mind that would not be put aside.

"Where is Jennifer?" he asked himself. "Carlotta too. Slade Salters won't have any pity if he finds her!"

He knew where Jennifer, at least, might be found. Moving toward the scattered fighting, he made for Jennifer's adobe. It was not far. There wasn't a light in the place, but that was only prudent, he thought. Reaching the door, he called anxiously:

"Jennifer! Are you there?"

There was no reply. Misgivings assailed him sharply. A loud knock went unanswered. Bursting in the door with a rush, he found the house was empty. The lean lines of his face drew tight.

Even as he returned to the open a woman's scream pierced the night. It came from a house a few feet away. Morningstar hurried there. He caught the glow of a lamp, and in its light, through the window, he saw not only Jennifer but Carlotta as well. Both girls had taken refuge in this place; evidently they were trying to barricade themselves in. Running along the side of the building, Jim heard the crashing thump of men trying to break in the door.

It smashed open just as he reached the porch corner. A man rushed in; another, hearing the stamp of Jim's boots, turned back. He brought his gun up as Morningstar leaped at him; it banged harmlessly. The next moment Jim's fist sent him sprawling headlong. It was Tip Slaughter. Jim stepped over him and got a flash of Salters confronting Sui Chen; Jennifer and Carlotta had fallen back behind the stout Oriental.

"One side, you!" Slade ripped out contemptuously. He slashed at Sui Chen with his gun barrel.

Standing a dozen feet behind him, Jim halted. Slade heard him. He may have thought it was Slaughter, but he paused momentarily. In that stiff silence Jim said flatly:

"Salters."

A shock ran through Slade. He recognized that voice. He did not turn at once, but his body stiffened. Slowly he began to wheel, his eyes wolfish in the handsome face. Before he fronted Morningstar squarely, his right arm partially concealed, he suddenly went for his other gun. Jim caught that move on the fly and his own play was instantaneous.

The two guns exploded almost as one. Salters' slug tore across Jim's arm. The latter's aim had been more accurate. Salters' eyes glazed. Suddenly he tottered drunkenly. He crumpled then, dead as he hit the floor.

"Jim! Jim! You are safe!"

It was Jennifer. Unmindful of Sui Chen and Carlotta, she ran to him and threw herself into

Morningstar's arms. "My dear, my dear!" they heard her broken murmur. "You might have been killed!"

There was undisguised pity in the look Sui Chen gave Carlotta. Neither could miss the significance of this moment. It spelled death for Carlotta's hopes where Jim Morningstar was concerned.

Emerging from the house five minutes later, Jim found the fight virtually over. Bronc Yeager had been taken after Sulphur drilled him through the shoulder. While the rest of the renegades battled fiercely, they had no leader after that. Mulhall soon had them rounded up. Looking them over, the district attorney had a few curt words to say as to their probable fate.

"I'll tell you better about that when I find out what's happened to my possemen," Huck told him. At the head of a dozen men, Morningstar among them, he led the way to the mine entrance, only to find his deputies free once more and the two men Salters had left to guard them already flown. The possemen's story proved Morningstar's surmise correct as to what had happened in the mine.

"You git your folks ready to move," Huck told Jim. "We'll be pullin' out in half an hour. We can put some miles behind us while it's cool."

Morningstar nodded woodenly. He watched the preparations for departure. The renegades were bound and made ready to travel under guard of Buck's possemen; food for two days was packed; Sulphur, Johnnie and Hap were plainly elated to be going. Even Jennifer must be making ready for the trip. Jim shook his head at the thought. Of all the whites in the valley, he alone must remain behind. He had never known how hard this hour would be to face until now.

It was an added shock to watch Bill Merriam's body being packed on a bronc. Not even the shadow of this man's pretensions stood between Jennifer and him now, but it meant nothing.

Stifling his despair, Morningstar turned away to wander beneath the trees. Only dimly through the misery that was in him was he aware of Sui Chen's friendly hail. The old man called a second time. "Jim, I must have a word with you."

Morningstar entered the now familiar office to find it heavy with the perfume Carlotta wore. It told him she had just quitted this room. He glanced inquiringly at Sui Chen. The latter was pacing the floor, his hands clasped behind his plump back. "Please sit down, Jim," he urged. And after a pause: "There are some reasons why I regret what I am about to say. They are not all selfish reasons, as you might presume. Some of them spring from my respect and fondness for you, others from my love for one who is as a daughter to me." He bowed his head reverently. "May Quam Yam have mercy on her."

His tone was calm, but Jim could sense the

emotional strain the man was under. "I hardly understand, Sui Chen," Morningstar said. "Let us be frank with each other."

"Yes," the old Oriental nodded, only half hearing. "We have a proverb to the effect that some there are who must walk alone," he went on, his train of thought unbroken. "It is the will of the gods," he sighed humbly. "Mere man can do nothing about it, even though he carries the green dragon."

He stopped his pacing abruptly and fastened his shrewd old eyes on Morningstar. "Jim, you have served us nobly. Believe me, this does not come easily, but Moy Quai is right: to hold you to your oath—to keep you from the woman you love—in view of all you have done for us, would be base ingratitude."

Morningstar pulled himself to his feet and stood gazing at him, amazed. "Sui Chen—am I to understand that I am relieved of my promise— that I am free to leave with the others?"

Sui Chen smiled. "So it means so much to you, my son?" He shook his wise old head. "I am not surprised. I, too, once was young." From a desk drawer he took a small envelope. "Between friends there must be no thought of paying for a favor—for a service well done. But I once promised you riches. Take this humble gift as a token of our regard for you. And may the god of luck go with you."

The unexpectedness of it overwhelmed Morningstar. He knew Carlotta had done this for him, but he little suspected what it cost her.

Quan Goon stepped into the room. "Miss Orme is waiting, Morningstar," he said soberly. "I have had your pony saddled. Mulhall and the others have started already."

The two Chinese bowed respectfully, once, twice, three times. It was their way of saying farewell. Jim couldn't let it go at that. He put out his hand and they shook hands in the white man's way.

Morningstar found Jennifer ready for the long ride. He sensed immediately that she had been informed that he was leaving with her. Her manner was subdued, wistful.

"We are leaving something here, Jim, that is fine and inspiring," she murmured softly. He nodded, too full for words.

Silver moonlight bathed Ping-an-shanku in a magic of its own. Peace had returned to the valley. It held them silent and thoughtful.

Emerging from the trees, Jim saw a figure silhouetted against the great rock that commanded a view of the trail out of the valley, someone who stood there motionless, waiting.

It was Carlotta, her face unreadable. Jennifer read the girl's heart plainly enough, however. "Jim—you wait here and say good-by to her," she whispered. "I'll ride on."

Carlotta did not turn at hearing his step behind her.

"You shouldn't have stopped," she said, her voice small and tense.

"I couldn't go without stopping, Carlotta. I know how much I owe you."

"It is nothing, Jim. We can't all win." She lifted her face to him, her eyes dark pools in the moonlight, and managed a smile. "The little dragon brought you happiness; that is something."

Morningstar caught her hands impulsively and felt the beat of life in her. That contact broke Carlotta's inner defenses. Suddenly she pressed close to him, her eyes wet. "Take me in your arms this once, Jim," she breathed ever so softly. "Let me have the feel of your lips on mine to remember."

Silence enfolded them during that long embrace. In the end Carlotta put him away from her. "Go now," she made herself say. "And please, Jim—don't look back!"

His face craggy, resolute, Jim fumbled for his stirrup, then swung up and started down the moonlit trail. Ahead he could see Jennifer, and he knew their trails lay together, not only across this valley and the next, but over the hills and ever beyond, sharing whatever life might bring them.